MOM-COM

MARIKA RAY

Mom-Com

First Edition: May 23, 2019

Special thanks to:

Cover Design by Laura Halloran
Editing by Lawrence Editing
Proofreading by Judy Zweifel
Proofreading by Shayne Ryder
Photography by Lindee Robinson
Model: Joshua Flaugher

DEDICATION

To every single mom and single dad out there...
I salute you.

MOM-COM

Can the single mom next door be the answer to his science experiment?

Jameson

   When my eight-year-old son starts asking question about love, I decide to use a magazine article on how to woo a woman to prove, once and for all, that romantic love doesn't exist. Companionship, habit, mild fondness, sure, but not that thing called love. I have my hypothesis ready and I'm dead set on experimenting on my new neighbor, the single mom who does the weirdest things.

   But my experiment goes awry in unexplainable ways...

Lily-Marie

   When dating apps fail me spectacularly, I decide to go old school and use a 1950s magazine I dug up at a yard sale to help find Mr. Right.

   Fifty Ways to Find a Husband.

   Sounds legit.

   Problem is, my new neighbor, Mr. Science Professor, keeps

blocking my attempts. And keeps losing his shirt. How does a book nerd have so many muscles anyway? Thing is, my kids like his son and we start spending a lot of time together, which is distracting me from my ultimate goal: to find a husband to sweep me off my feet and be a good father to my kids.

Things get comical quick when my best friend records everything in her daily newspaper column. I can't help but wonder if single moms like me can actually catch a husband. Or will this Mom-Com go viral as an epic train wreck?

Book two in the Reality of Love series.

1

ily-Marie

I clicked the door shut behind me, wishing I could slam it instead and get out some of the frustration bubbling inside me. With my two kids asleep in their beds—dear God, please say they were asleep—a soft click would have to do. That's why moms drank wine. It was silent, tasty, and calmed the daily frustrations that chafed almost as badly as the Spanx trying to hold in my pooch-y belly those same kids were responsible for.

We couldn't have tantrums, so we drank. Sue me.

"Gabby?" I whisper-yelled into my house.

My lifelong best friend was babysitting for me tonight so I could "enjoy" a night out with a guy I'd connected with on Kinder, the latest dating app that promised "solid relationships with just one click!" More like false promises and nightmares. Bejeezus, why were people so weird? Was it too much to ask to be swept off one's feet by a dashing prince? Although, I guess that wasn't Kinder's fault. Maybe I should blame the company I happened to work for. I mean, they kind of sold me—even as a little girl—on the idea of a prince saving me with one perfect kiss.

"Hey, how did it go?" Gabby came around the corner, rubbing her eyes. She checked the watch on her wrist, frowning.

I hung my jacket up on the hook by the door and moved farther into the house.

"Yeah, it's early, I know. Sorry to interrupt your nap. It was a lukewarm date right up until he whipped out his phone over the appetizers and showed me—and I'm not kidding you—at least thirty dick pics. Apparently, there's an art form for taking just the right one, did you know?" Her jaw dropped open and I continued. That joy needed to be spread. "Because, as I learned, lighting, angle, level of excitement, the temperature in the room. Those are all things that can positively or negatively affect the end result. Which. He. Showed. Me."

My eyes glazed over and I full-body shivered just recalling the things I'd seen. Gabby snapped her mouth closed and hustled around me to the kitchen, pulling down a bottle of wine from the top cabinet that had seen better days. At some point I'd get around to refacing my cabinets. Tonight was not that day.

"I know what this calls for. Tonight's a merlot night." She pulled out two glasses and got to work on the cork.

I sank into a bar stool and pushed the kids' stack of graded homework out of the way. "God bless you." My shoes, the ones I only pulled out for dates because they killed my feet, were kicked off in a frenzy. And then, only because we were such good friends and I had enough dirt on her to last a lifetime, I reached up under my dress and peeled off the Spanx so I could breathe.

"Oh, that's nice..." I whispered, sitting back down and accepting the glass she held out to me. The first sip went down the hatch and I could feel the layer of ick he'd left on me with his detailed pictures sliding off my skin, hopefully never to be seen again.

"That's truly the most disgusting thing I've heard recently. And I just babysat your eight-year-old son, who thought it was fun to make slime and smear it all over his skin like he was a mutant lizard shedding his winter coat." Gabby sat on the stool next to me, her long black hair always so perfect, even though she'd just woken up after babysitting the hellion spawn of mine I loved so dearly.

I cringed. "Ah, conned you into making slime again, huh?"

She shrugged. "It made him happy and you know I can't say no to my godchildren." She raised her glass and we clinked them together before taking another healthy swig. "So, fill me in. How have the other dates gone?"

Gabby was a hotshot columnist for the LA Times, writing a modern-day advice column, similar to Ann Landers, but with a younger perspective. She was busy all the time, but still found time to encourage—nag—me about going on dates with men I met online.

I'd been single for two years, but was just now feeling like dating men was something I was ready for. I'd only been with my ex, having dated him all through high school and most of college before we had kids together. We never officially got married, and that was something that had always bothered me. Call me old-fashioned, but I really wanted to wear a white dress and show off my sparkling diamond engagement ring. Which, if these recent dates were any indication, wouldn't be happening any time soon. My cabinets would be getting that remodel before I was a Mrs.

"Oh God, Gabby. It's so bad out there. Seriously. Count yourself lucky you have a man already." I rubbed my forehead, smearing the makeup I'd so carefully applied just a few hours before. She didn't say anything, so I kept spewing, the words leaking out uncensored. This was what I needed. Time with my bestie. Total therapy. "So, I went on that mid-day coffee date last week and I should have known better. He never showed. And here's the kicker: his *mom* showed up to tell me he couldn't make it."

Gabby drew her head back sharply. "No!"

I slapped a hand down on the counter and immediately winced at the noise it made, hurrying on in a whisper. "Yes! She said he'd wrecked her car that morning and she took away his cell phone as punishment. Then she proceeded to tell me how wonderful he normally is and that I should call him in two days when she gave him back his cell phone."

Gabby's giggle turned into a full-out belly laugh. She abandoned her wine glass on the counter and bent over, muffling her laugh with her knees.

"It's not funny!" I whisper-yelled at the top of her head. "Besides, you're going to want to hear what happened with my lunch date."

Her head whipped up and she swiped the tears from her wide eyes. "It gets worse?"

I took the time to top off my glass before answering. She laughed at me. She could wait a minute or two before I told her more. "As I was saying, I had a lunch date last week too. I showed up, he showed up. He was just as attractive as his picture, so things were looking good, right? Next thing I know, he's telling me all about his last fight with his ex-girlfriend. And I mean details! Like his favorite red sundress she was wearing, and the way she called him an asshole under her breath, which she knows he hates. By the time my salad showed up, I was ready to shovel it down and get the hell out of there."

"Wow, Lil, that's crazy. I wish I could say that's abnormal, but there are some crazy-ass people out there." Gabby looked at me sympathetically. She got a lot of crazies writing in and asking her for advice on bizarre life situations, so I knew she understood.

"But that's not even the end of it." I placed my glass on the counter. I needed two hands for this. "By the time I ate my salad, he'd let the cat out of the bag that he and his girlfriend were *still together*. They hadn't actually broken up. I was out on a lunch date helping a guy cheat on his girlfriend."

"Oh, honey..." Gabby looked a little green. That was an area we'd always agreed on: cheating was never okay. Not ever.

"But wait!" I stopped talking and burst out laughing. "Oh my God! I sound like an infomercial. 'But wait, there's more!'" Gabby laughed with me and then I finished it. "So, naturally, I hop up like my chair's on fire and head out the door. He follows me all the way to my car and tries to hug me. I push him off me, but his hand is stuck in my purse. The fucker was trying to pickpocket me on our cheating date!"

Gabby jumped off the stool and looked ready to fight the dude right there on the spot. "What did you do?"

"I slapped his hand away from my purse, kicked him in the nuts, and drove off."

We bumped fists and settled back down on our stools to sip our wine and calm down.

"I feel highly compelled to write about this. You know that, right?" Gabby looked at me, pleading with her dark eyes.

I shook my head. "I'm sorry, but my pathetic dating life can't be in your column. My fragile ego can't handle it."

"Even if it's anonymous?"

"Even if it's anonymous. *I'd* know, Gabby." I sighed. "After Shawn, I just don't know if I can handle more of a spotlight on my singlehood, you know?"

Her hand rubbed my back. "I know. I promise I won't write anything. The last thing I want to do is discourage you from getting back out there. Shawn wasn't your forever, but your forever is out there somewhere waiting for you. I just know it." She pulled me into a side hug. "I'm proud of you, Lil."

"Thanks, Gabriella. I'm proud of me for trying too. When Shawn left, I was shocked. I thought we'd be together forever. I never envisioned being a single mom and trying to date thirtysomethings who were passed over or left behind. They all have this desperation that clings to them like a bad odor." Oh jeez, I needed to put down the wine before I got any more poetic.

"What I'm trying to say is I just don't think this app thing is going to work. The kind of guy I'm looking for doesn't live with his mama and he surely doesn't need to pickpocket me to pay his rent. I need a man who sweeps me off my feet and only has eyes for me. He'll take one look at me and my children and want to put a big rock on my finger. And if he's really awesome, he'll snuggle with me and watch Disney princess movies. Is that too much to ask?"

Gabby went surprisingly serious on me, even though I handed her the perfect opportunity to tease me about my princess obsession. "No, that's not too much to ask. In fact, I think we should have always been demanding that. Maybe our problem has always been not asking for enough." Before I could examine that nugget of wisdom or ask how things were going with Hew, her boyfriend, she hopped off the stool and started gathering her things. "Gotta go, girlie. Got words to write and hours to toss and turn before my alarm goes off."

I made a mental note to sit her down soon and see if things were rocky with her and Hewitt. They'd been together for years now, maybe not blissfully happy, but steady nonetheless. She hadn't said anything outright, but my best friend radar was beeping. Something wasn't right with her and I intended to get to the bottom of it.

I walked her out and made sure she got on the road safe. Then I locked up, turned out lights, and headed up to kiss my babies goodnight. They wouldn't remember, but I couldn't help myself. They gave me gray hairs, but I loved them fiercely. Sleep wouldn't come if I didn't check on them and give them the kisses they wouldn't normally stand still for long enough when they were awake.

Clark was flat on his back, arms and legs spread like he'd squeezed every last drop of life out of the day before flopping back on his mattress and conking out. I pulled the sheets from under his legs and covered him up, my movements not even stirring him. He was still so small at eight years old, even as he tried to act like the man of the house with his father gone. Sure, he saw his dad every other weekend, but in between those times, he was trying to act older. Why, I didn't know, but I hoped he stayed a kid for as long as he could.

I tiptoed into Milly's room, skipping over the wood board that creaked. She slept light and was hard to creep in on. There'd already been some near misses on Christmas Eve when I'd been trying to get her presents under the tree from Santa and she'd heard me.

My beautiful girl had big, blond curls that reminded me of myself at that age. I'd learned to control them with products, but on a five-year-old, they were adorable and wild. I brushed the barest of kisses on her forehead and backed away slowly.

It was moments like these that made everything right in my world. I had my kids. I had my health. Everything would be fine.

In my own bedroom, I put on my cotton pajama pants and ratty, old tank top before snuggling under the covers and clicking on the TV with the remote. I hit play and smiled as the opening credits to *Sleeping Beauty* floated softly through the speakers. I was the proud owner of every Disney princess movie on DVD. Some women needed Ambien to sleep. I needed happy ever afters and Prince Charming.

The melodic notes of "I Wonder" flowed over me as Aurora sang to the forest animals. My eyes began to blink shut as I commiserated with her. She wondered where her someone was and so did I.

Fumbling with the remote, I finally shut it off and drifted to sleep, visions of princesses and handsome princes filling my head. Except in my dreams, one of the handsome men was for little, old me. He picked me up and swung me around at a fancy ball, my children on the sidelines smiling from ear to ear. A diamond ring sat on my finger as he pulled me in for a kiss...

ameson

"Dad! Where are you?"

I heard Stein's muffled voice as I was digging through yet another box of clothing, looking for my favorite sweater.

"I'm in the closet!" I shouted back.

I saw an edge of forest green and grabbed it, pulling it out from the bottom, spilling clothes out onto the ground around me. Moving wasn't for the faint of heart, as I was finding out. I couldn't find a damn thing since we'd moved two days ago. Maybe it had to do with the way I labeled the boxes. Instead of writing what was in each one, I'd simply put which room it was to go into. Great on moving day, not so great when you were staring at twenty identical boxes in your bedroom and wondering where your favorite sweater was on Monday morning, the first day of school.

"I can't find my lunch sack, Dad." Stein was now right behind me, his little face scrunched up comically, like his missing lunch bag was the worst thing that could happen. But I guess when you're eight and it's your first day of second grade at a new school, having everything perfect was paramount.

Ruffling the fluffy light brown hair on top of his head, I stood up and motioned for him to follow me. "No problem, kiddo. I know I saw it in the kitchen somewhere."

I hadn't, but damn if I wasn't going to find it so he could have one less thing to worry about. It was my fault we had to move in the middle of the school year. When Pacific Coast College called with an open position to head their science department, I really couldn't say no. It was the step I needed, both in pay and in position, to eventually land myself a job at one of the University of California campuses. Those jobs were coveted and rare. I intended to be on staff at UC before I was forty. Yes, I had six years before I hit the big four-oh, but even so, I'd be pushing it to hit my goal.

"Can you make my peanut butter sandwich with bananas and honey like Mom does it?"

The mention of his mom was like a dagger to my heart. Not because I held any feelings for her anymore, or maybe ever, but because I knew he kept her up on a pedestal. No little boy should have to beg for his mother's attention, but that's what Stein has always had to do with her. He overcompensated by talking about her all the time, and even though I was an adult and could see where the comments were stemming from, the constant reminder of his obsession with her was hard to take. Especially when I was the only parent rearranging my life every day to take care of him like he deserved.

"Sure, buddy. Why don't you look through these boxes over here while I make your lunch?" I kept one eye on him as he picked his way through a box of kitchen utensils and one eye on making his lunch to his specifications. No sandwich crust, one cookie, fifteen green grapes, two string cheeses. I was hoping this finicky phase passed quickly, but given the genetics involved, I feared it might stick around for life. Like father, like son.

Lunch packed in the newly found lunch bag, we made a mad dash to brush teeth and layer on jackets. Yes, it was Southern California, but January could still be cold. Dress like winter in the morning, but have summer layers on underneath in case the sun came out full force in the afternoon.

Right as we got to the front door to leave, I knelt down and tugged him over to stand in front of me. His backpack was nearly as big as him. I looked him straight in his gray eyes, so like mine it was spooky.

"It's a big day for both of us, buddy. We're going to make new friends today and learn lots. Sound like a plan?" My heart was oddly pounding in my chest. It was like it was the first day of kindergarten all over again.

"You're going to do great today, Dad, don't worry." He put his little hand on my shoulder and I nearly confessed the secret that all parents have: we'd literally do anything for these tiny little humans. The alarm on my phone went off, breaking the moment and keeping me from spilling my guts.

"Time to roll, Stein." I stood up and ushered him out the door to my trusty Volvo. The safety rating was killer on that thing and with precious cargo on board, I didn't trust anything without a five-star rating by the National Highway Traffic Safety Administration.

He was just about buckled in when I heard the front door burst open next door. Out flowed two kids and one frazzled mother. They were putting on jackets as they hustled to their SUV, with the mom stopping to pick something up from the driveway.

"Ooh! Look, kids! It's heads up. You know what that means." She looked positively radiant, like a heads-up penny was some kind of omen for good luck, when in reality, it had been her own mistake that had caused her to drop it carelessly in the first place.

I shook my head at such utter foolishness. Even the notion of "luck" was just a simplified explanation for probability working out in your favor. Random things were usually not so random when you looked at the events that led to them. People who found "lucky" pennies were also found to be more apt to look at the ground when they walked, which led to finding more pennies because they were looking at the location where pennies would naturally be found. Luck? I didn't think so.

I slid into the car and got the heater going while I watched them do the same. Regardless of her lack of sense when it came to luck, she was an attractive lady with her navy blue dress and wool coat. Her blond hair was curling down her back, a few pieces on the sides pinned back artfully. Her son looked to be about Stein's age, so I made a mental note to introduce myself later.

As we drove to Stein's new school, he kept up a steady stream of chatter from the back seat. I answered here and there, my thoughts darting around to all the things I needed to accomplish today on my first day at my new school too.

"Hey, Dad?"

"Yeah, buddy?"

"Did you love Mom when you had me?"

My brain froze and so did my whole body. Luckily we were stopped at a red light or who knows what ditch I would have driven into. Every horror story of having the birds and the bees talk with your kid swooped through my head. Was that what he was asking?

"Why do you ask?" I was careful to keep my tone neutral.

"Well, you said you met Mom at college, so maybe with this new college you might meet another girl and fall in love with her. Right?"

I shook my head to clear the cobwebs, grateful at least we'd staved off the sex talk for another day. "First of all, I don't know if romantic love really exists. It's biologically programmed in most species to care for and demonstrate love for their offspring. But only a few species display any inkling of affection for a mate. If anything, some species keep a mate to help out either with offspring or simply for survival, not because of any feelings. So, I can't say I was ever in love with your mom. I cared for her, of course, but love? I don't think that really exists, buddy. In fact, one of these days, I'll prove it to you."

Glancing in the rearview mirror, I saw his face pinched, his gaze taking in the sidewalk as we zoomed through the neighborhood by his school.

"I don't know what a shpee-zee is, but I think I know what you're saying. So, if people don't really love each other like that then why do they get married?"

I bit my lip to keep the smile off my face. He was so damn cute. Here I was spouting off about species and biology and he just wanted to know if I was going to find some woman at my new workplace and disrupt his life.

"I think people like companionship. They like to do things together, so they get married or live together, that's all. But don't worry, Stein. I have no intention of bringing home a woman from my new school."

"Hey, that lady from next door is right behind us!" His attention span was that of a squirrel, always off to the next thing.

My gaze shifted to the rearview mirror and I saw her expressive face steering her big SUV into the parking lot of the school, just like Stein said. Guess her kids went to this school too. Maybe Stein and her son could be friends. A little bit of weight lifted from my shoulders at the thought.

"Bye, Dad!"

As soon as my car came to a stop, Stein unlocked his door and hopped out, swinging his backpack with him. I chuckled at his enthusiasm, realizing this wasn't at all like kindergarten when he clung to my leg and begged me to stay. I tracked his progress into the school yard and then saw him approach the neighbor kid.

A car honked behind me and I rushed to put my car in gear. I guess my pretty neighbor was in a hurry. I'd learned quickly enough that school drop-off zones were like a war zone, every mom and dad for themselves. No time for loving glances and wistful goodbyes.

I pondered my conversation with Stein while I drove to PCC. He didn't seem too concerned with a woman in my life, which made me relieved, but also adrift. How was I supposed to field questions to the satisfaction of a curious eight-year-old when I didn't know the answer myself? I'd felt affection—and a lot of lust—for his mother back when we were in college, but I definitely wouldn't call it love. When we split, I was ambivalent at best, which didn't scream the L-word.

My brain was hatching a crazy idea: an experiment to prove once and for all that romantic love didn't exist. I was a scientist. Proving things was my life's work. This would be no different and it would finally lay to rest that question for Stein. And myself, if I was being honest.

A parking space with my name printed on a metal placard bolted to a post was waiting for me when I pulled into the new campus. My fingers itched to take a picture of it, but who would I send it to? My dad, the esteemed professor at Stanford? I didn't think a parking space at a community college rated a picture. And I didn't do that social media stuff, so what was the point?

By the time I found my office and got settled in, I had to rush back out and find the classroom where I'd be teaching a Biology 101 class that semester. Yes, I was now the head of the department, but I still taught three classes. I was happy with that arrangement as it kept my feet on the ground and my safety goggles in a science lab every week.

After class with a delightful load of new, eager students—hopefully my sarcasm was apparent—I hightailed it back to my office for lunch and then an afternoon of getting my office organized.

The Star Wars theme song blared from the bottom of my satchel not long after I sat down at my desk. I fished it out and answered, knowing it was my dad from his ring tone.

"Father. Happy Monday."

"Greetings to you as well, my son." He chuckled, loving the act of Mr. Proper when we both knew it was just a matter of time before the f-bombs came flying. "You'll never guess what I'm working on."

"You're using the Advanced Light Source to dissect DNA damage that leads to RNA transcription errors, thus leading to curing cancer," I deadpanned.

"Don't be ridiculous," he boomed. "I'm using the ALS to create high-capacity lithium battery electrodes so I can make millions of dollars and retire before I'm dead."

"Careful. Your capitalism is showing..."

"Enough bullshit, Jameson," he huffed, obviously done with my teasing. "I'm calling because I had a moment of weakness this weekend. I was feeling old, so I went through all those boxes in the attic you call a fire hazard and decided to put together an online album of sorts about my parents, about my life, and then you and Stein can add to it over time as well. Basically, I'm creating a living, breathing time capsule, thus making myself immortal. Impressed yet?"

I rolled my eyes. That was so my father. "Better than your decapitated head in a cryo chamber somewhere."

"That's not a bad idea either, but I'm still alive and kicking right now, so I'll stick to the time capsule. Anyway, I came across some articles yesterday in an old box that I think you should see. I scanned them and emailed them to you. I'll wait."

Silence ensued and I realized he wanted me to log into my email and read it right now. No one said no to Mr. MacMillan without the time and energy to fight the battle that transpired. I had neither the time nor the energy, so I opened my laptop and found his email.

I scanned over the attached documents and barked out a laugh when the meaning hit me. "Are you serious with this?"

"As a heart attack."

I scrubbed a hand over my face. Maybe I needed glasses after all. I couldn't believe what my eyes were seeing. An article, written by Loni Sanders, the pseudonym my grandmother used in her magazine column days, was sitting in my inbox, the title mocking me.

Fifty Ways to Find a Wife

"I—What—" I cleared my throat and tried again. "Why did you send this to me?"

And then I heard it. The low-pitched wheeze that signaled my eardrums were about to split wide-open. I pulled the phone away from my ear just in time as he let out the loudest guffaw known to man. I was surprised my phone case didn't crack under the pressure.

"Breathe, Dad." If I knew the man, and I did, his face was bright red and he was laughing so hard he wasn't breathing. Just wind whistling through his throat in gasps and spurts.

"It's just..." He cackled again, his words coming out in between fits of laughter. "So ridiculous...who would follow...I can't believe...my own mother...wrote such shit!"

Then he was off in another fit of laughter and I couldn't help the smile that tugged on my lips. His laugh was highly contagious if a bit alarming. And he had a point: the article was crazy. I read through the list of fifty ways while I gave my father some time to calm himself. Granny actually had a few really interesting ones, like *If your girl is ill, call from work to check on her health.*

That sounded like genuinely good advice. It was always a good idea to show you cared. Maybe *Be courageous, don't be a sissy* was a little harsh, but I saw her point. Women loved a dashing hero, right?

"I'll forward any more gems I come across." Rustling could be heard on the other end of the line. I was guessing it was my father wiping the tears from his ruddy cheeks.

"Yeah, okay, sounds good." I hung up, distracted. I couldn't stop reading the list. And as I read, a lightbulb flared to life in my head. Maybe that lucky penny my neighbor picked up this morning meant good luck for me instead of her. Because everything was coming together. I'd started my new job, Stein started a new school, and I had the perfect idea to prove my theory correct.

I'd unleash the fifty ways to find a wife on my next-door neighbor and when it failed spectacularly, I'd prove once and for all that romantic love doesn't exist.

For Stein.

And for me.

Brilliant.

ily-Marie

A car door slamming woke me from my dreamless slumber. Since my kids were with their father this weekend, I'd cozied up in my bed last night with a good Hallmark movie and didn't set an alarm. Pure heaven to sleep as long as I wanted—minus the car door slamming—waking to the sun streaming through my sheer curtains. The week had flown by with the kids back to school and everyone finally getting work done now that the holidays were over. A few extra hours of sleep was just what I needed.

I threw back the covers and stretched, finding my slippers by the bed. It was cold still in Southern California in January and the tile floor was freezing in the mornings. Shuffling into the kitchen to get my first cup of coffee brewing, I peered out the window and saw an unfamiliar car out front. It was parked between my house and the new next-door neighbor.

Feeling like a busybody, I went over to the window in the

front living room and peeked through the blinds. A tall brunette stood by the car, her arms folded and an irritated expression on her face. Then my tall neighbor came down the walkway with his son practically jumping out of his shoes. I'd learned earlier this week that the little boy went to my kids' school. This exact scene played out every other weekend in my life for the last two years, so I recognized it for what it was: a divorced parent hand-off.

That reminded me. I needed to bake some cookies this weekend and take the kids over tomorrow night after their dad dropped them back home. We needed to introduce ourselves to the new neighbors. I searched for a Post-it note in the kitchen and wrote it down on my to-do list. That was the only way I'd remember. I had Post-it notes all over the house, decorating every surface like a demented Pottery Barn catalog. Grabbing my coffee, I moved back to the front window for more free entertainment.

My neighbor walked back up the walkway after his ex's car drove away. He had that familiar slump to his shoulders. Poor guy. I didn't know how fresh his split was, but it was hard at first to see them leave. Don't get me wrong, I still missed my kids when they were with their father, but I was also enjoying the perks. Like sleeping in on a Saturday morning with no one but myself to get ready.

My gaze trailed absentmindedly over his pressed slacks and dark cranberry sweater. His outfit could have been worn by an eighty-year-old for all the fashion sense it exuded, but his strong jawline and gorgeous dark hair kept him in a decidedly younger age bracket.

I tilted my head, seeing him from a different angle. Yep, with a trendier outfit on, he could look quite dashing. Handsome, actually, if you dug the moody professor type.

He was confuzzling. Who wore slacks and a sweater like that so early on a Saturday morning? I usually met my ex at the door with my pajamas and yesterday's hair in a messy bun. I'd briefly considered sprucing myself up early on and showing him what he gave up, but quickly decided that would take far too much effort that was better spent finding my Prince Charming. This guy? He was really taking things to the next level if he was trying to impress his ex.

I went to sip my coffee and found my mug empty. Time to stop snooping on my neighbor, get another cup of coffee, and get started on what was one of my favorite pastimes. Saturday mornings were for yard sales! Since my left hand was busy holding my mug, I was forced to do a one-handed jazz hands motion there by myself in my kitchen. My kids weren't there to groan at my mom-moves, so I really put some muscle into it. I absolutely loved finding deals. Plus, I fully believed that one man's trash was another man's treasure. Or in this case, woman's.

Rushing through my routine—after all, it was Saturday, how fancy did I need to be—I was out the door in record time. No sign of my single neighbor, but then again, I wasn't exactly looking for him either.

By the time I'd made it to my third yard sale in a ten-mile radius of my house, I was about to call it a day. I'd found an old book I'd always wanted to read, a Disney princess ornament I didn't have already, and a sterling silver nut cracker. Like an actual tool that would crack nuts, not a red soldier. Figured I might need a nut cracker if I went on any more dates. Get it? Nut cracker? I snorted to myself as I got out of the car and perused the offerings at the front. That was a pretty bad joke, I admit, but then again, my dates had been pretty bad jokes too.

This yard sale sported a lot of furniture, but I really didn't need any of that. I was about to leave in defeat when I spotted a tall stack of old magazines. A small smile lit my face when I saw they were Prevention magazines I remembered reading when I visited my grandparents' house as a small child. I flipped through the one at the top and then the second one. A title of an article caught my eye and I scrambled to get back to the right page.

The sounds of the people milling about faded away and all I saw were the words *Fifty Ways to Find a Husband.* I scanned the list like a kid at the donut counter. I devoured each one and wanted to take a screen shot to reference back. Then I realized the ridiculousness of that statement as this was paper and ink, written long before smartphones or even desktop computers.

Instead, I dug in my pocket and found the quarter I needed to buy the magazine, which I realized was highway robbery for an old magazine, but desperate times and all that. Once I'd paid, I hustled to my car and slid inside to read in private.

"Hot damn, Ms. Sanders. You're an angel," I whispered to the empty car, in awe of the drops of wisdom this woman had imparted to the world before I was even born. Okay, wisdom might be pushing it. I mean, she had some interesting ones that were more comical than wise.

Learn to paint...set up an easel outside of an engineering school.

I was all for thinking outside the box, but that one didn't even make sense. Could you imagine if I tried that in today's era? I'd probably be arrested for trespassing or given a psych evaluation.

Dropping the handkerchief still works.

Say what now? That one would probably need to be modified. Maybe dropping a pen or something would work better. Hell, I didn't even own a handkerchief, so a pen would have to do.

That thought stopped me up short. I raised my head and blinked, taking in the world around me. What was I thinking? Was I actually considering attempting these fifty ways to find a husband?

"You've lost it now, Lily-Marie." I laid the magazine down on the passenger seat and started the car. I needed to pull my head out of the 1950s and get real. A modern woman didn't find a man by turning into a simpering airhead and playing these games. Did she?

I pulled away from the curb and hung a left to head back home, my mind swirling. I'd been trying the dating apps, which according to Gabby and quite a few of my single coworkers, were supposed to be the number one way to find a match. And so far all that had netted me was a headache and a solo trip to the adult toy store.

Those weren't the men I wanted. I needed a man to sweep me off my feet like they did in the movies or romance novels. A man who could fix my car, provide for our family, and rock my world at night when the kids went to bed. Those kinds of men didn't seem to be on dating apps.

So maybe Gabby was wrong. Maybe my coworkers were wrong.

Maybe what I needed was some old-fashioned advice from Loni Sanders, circa 1959.

Couldn't be any worse than the men I'd met through Kinder, that was for damn sure. By the time I swung into my driveway, I'd convinced myself to give the list a shot. Maybe not all fifty ways, but at least a few. At the very worst, there was no harm in it, right?

So, I slid into a chair at my kitchen table with the Prevention magazine and my spiral notebook side by side and laid out a plan. Some of the fifty were flat-out ridiculous and I would skip over them.

Go to a football game and get lost.

I scrunched up my nose. Who gets lost at a football game? Better to streak across the football field in my birthday suit. Now *that* was more likely to win myself some husband potential! Then I remembered the twenty pounds I kept meaning to lose and I tossed the idea aside in favor of less revealing things. Also, I didn't want to get arrested. That would be a bad thing to have to inform my young children of. Sorry to miss your play, darlings, but Mom's in the slammer.

Take up golf.

I'd rather die a thousand deaths than hit a ball with a stick. That one wasn't making the cut. Of course, there were others that wouldn't work, simply because I was living half a century after she'd written the article. No payphone booths to get tangled up with a good-looking man. Or harpsichords I could borrow to impress the gentlemen with my strumming skills. Ah, well, fifty was probably too many to tackle anyway.

Decision made, a list of twenty seemed more realistic. I got busy transcribing the ones I planned to try out in my notebook. If I made a goal of two per week, I would have a nice long line of men waiting outside my door, I just knew it.

Once I had my twenty all laid out, I grabbed my phone to call Gabby to tell her about my change in plans. I wasn't going modern with dating apps, I was going retro with vintage dating advice from Prevention magazine. She'd be thrilled, I was sure.

"Hey, Lil, what's up?"

"Gabby?" I could barely contain my excitement. You know that feeling you have at the top of the roller coaster? My heart was pounding and I could barely catch my breath. I was exhilarated. "You're never gonna guess what I'm doing."

Twenty Ways to Find a Husband:

1. *Get a dog and walk it*
2. *Have your car break down in strategic places (fire station!)*
3. *Be nice to everybody—they may have an eligible brother/son*
4. *Flirt even with ugly men...they're the ones who will be faithful*
5. *Sit next to men, not women, in public social situations*
6. *Stumble when you walk by him, so he knows you're there*
7. *Wear a Band-Aid, men will ask what happened*
8. *Stand in a corner and cry softly, he'll come over to see what's wrong*

9. *Learn how to bake tasty apple pies...bring one to all areas where eligible bachelors go*
10. *Accidentally drop your purse/bag and have contents fly all over the street so he'll help you*
11. *If you look good in sweaters, wear them more often*
12. *Go on a diet if you need to*
13. *When on a date, order a rare steak*
14. *Don't whine—girls who whine stay on the vine!*
15. *Don't talk about how many children you want (the cows may have already left the barn on that one...)*
16. *Learn to sew and wear something you made yourself*
17. *Very early in your dating, why not get a favorite song that you both regard as "your song"?*
18. *Resist the urge to make him over—before marriage that is!*
19. *Clip and mail him a funny cartoon you think he'd like*
20. *Make and sell toupees—Bald men are easy catches!*

4

ameson

Today was the day. I was ready. I'd constructed my hypothesis, written out my predictions, and designed the experiment the best I could. I didn't have the luxury of a control group to test the effect of my independent variable, but I did write out all the steps of my experiment in great detail, going so far as to type up the ways I'd attempt to woo my neighbor. Laminating the list was a little over the top, but I didn't like to take any chances once an experiment was underway. What if I spilled my coffee?

Twenty Ways to Find a Wife:

    1. *Be involved in civic affairs*
    2. *Be athletic*

3. *Be helpful around the house*
4. *Do unexpected nice things often (flowers, candy, etc.)*
5. *Be well-read*
6. *Have a good, steady profession*
7. *Learn to dance, especially the waltz*
8. *Don't scold children too harshly in front of an attractive female*
9. *Suggest going clothes shopping on your date*
10. *Prepare your own breakfast or even breakfast for her!*
11. *Be neat in appearance—shoes shined, hair combed, shirt pressed*
12. *Be courageous, not a sissy*
13. *Eat whatever is served without complaining*
14. *Give swoon-worthy movie kisses, not a peck on the cheek*
15. *If girlfriend is ill, call from work to inquire about her health*
16. *Compliment her incessantly*
17. *Don't be a bookworm, talk to her!*
18. *Hold her coat, open doors for her, help her into and out of chair, stand up when she leaves the table*
19. *Pop a button off your shirt so she can sew it on for you*
20. *Keep tools in your car so if you see her on the side of the road, you can swoop in and fix her car*

When Stein's mother had called the night before and asked to spend the weekend with him, my first instinct was to say no. She'd missed the last two times she'd been scheduled to spend time with him. Plus, how about giving me advanced notice, huh? But then I saw the laminated list on the table, which was just the motivation I needed to tell her yes. Of course, I hadn't told Stein until this morning when I'd texted her and she'd confirmed she was in the car, on the way over. I needed some adult time to get started on my love experiment.

When I turned around to walk back into the house after making sure Stein was in the car with his seatbelt fastened, I saw some movement in the front window of my neighbor's house. Considering I'd seen her kids getting picked up the night before, I knew she was the only one in the house. Plus, the bright blond hair shining through the glass had given her away.

So, she was spying on me, huh? That would do just fine to start my experiment.

I went back inside and changed out of the clothes I'd just gotten into. Step number two on my list was begging to be enacted. Despite the fact I usually had my nose in a science textbook or something equally intellectual, I did enjoy athletic pursuits. A few years back I joined a colleague for a bike ride and found myself hooked. I was hoping my tight cycling jersey would be just the thing to turn the lady's head.

Once my shorts and shirt were on, I had a tough decision to make. I could go out barefoot, but that didn't seem like the best idea when it was fifty-five degrees outside, but the only footwear appropriate would be my cycling cleats. Anyone who'd ever worn bike shoes knew those suckers were hard to walk in. They had a stiff sole and a metal cleat smack-dab in the middle, which made for comfortable riding, but walking in them left the rider looking like a drunk flamingo. You couldn't really push off like in a normal gait with the metal cleat hindering natural movement. Not really the impression I wanted to make, but barefoot seemed even worse, so cleats it was.

I went out through the garage and grabbed my bike off the hook I installed that week. Rolling it out to the driveway that butted up against my neighbor's property, I flipped the bike over and prepared to grease my chain in full view of her front window. I even zipped the front zipper down a bit on my shirt, making sure my manly chest was displayed to its full advantage. I didn't want to brag, but I had a muscle or two thanks to good ol' Dad's genetics.

Before long I saw the blind move on the front window again. My heart started pounding in my chest, but I remained steady, pretending my whole focus was on my bike. I was just spraying some more lubricant on the chain when her front door cracked open and she sauntered out.

"Oh!" Her hand fluttered to her chest, like she was surprised to see me there.

I had to admit, her acting skills were quite good. If I hadn't seen her spying on me from the front window just moments ago, I would have believed I'd startled her. Instead, I smiled at her and lifted my hand in a wave. Time to start my experiment.

"Hello! I'm the new neighbor," I called out.

I proceeded to bobble the can of lube like an inexperienced scientist when my gaze met hers for the first time. Her blond hair was a gorgeous tumble of beach-y curls, longer than most women wore their hair these days. And the curves didn't stop there. I tried to keep my eyes on hers, but the lure of her generous breasts, tight waist, and flared hips were too much for my self-control. I did a quick scan—enough to tell me I was talking to one of the most attractive females I'd ever encountered—and then I gritted my teeth and forced my gaze to stay on hers.

She walked toward me, those hips shifting and swaying, taunting me. But then a smile split her face and I was entranced. Those lips were made to grin like that: wide, open, genuine.

When she was on the other side of my bike, close enough to touch, close enough to smell her flowery perfume, I forgot all about my experiment. Forgot completely that observing my subject and cataloguing all her features wasn't a necessary part of testing my hypothesis. Because at that moment, it felt most definitely necessary. Maybe even imperative.

"Hello. I'm Lily-Marie."

Her throaty voice washed over me, swirling with her perfume in teasing my senses. I reached out my right hand automatically, expecting a quick handshake as was customary when meeting someone for the first time. She glanced down at my hand, then back up at me, her smile slipping. A moment of awkward silence hung there before I also looked down and saw that I had a greasy can of lubricant in my hand. The hand that was outstretched, almost sullying Lily-Marie's blouse.

"Oh! Sorry." I quickly dropped the can, but jumped again when the impact of the can hitting the ground shot a stream of lube into the air, narrowly missing Lily-Marie's boots.

I wasn't a man to blush, but I felt the heat anyway, the burn of embarrassment creeping its way up my spine. I wasn't one for crude innuendo, but nobody could have missed that obvious enactment. She finally slipped her hand into mine and gave it a firm shake.

"Wow, that was a narrow miss." She laughed and I tried to follow suit. "So, Lance, what are you doing out here?"

My lips pinched together. "Who's Lance?"

The smile was back, lighting up the conversation when it most badly needed it. "You, silly. Lance Armstrong? Famous bike rider?" When I still looked perplexed, she spelled it out for me. "You haven't told me your name."

Ah! She was telling a joke. I got it. I totally got it. "Good one!" I laughed again, amazing even myself when it came out sounding like one of my father's wheezy guffaws. "It's Jameson. Jameson MacMillan." Great, now I sounded like James Bond.

"Nice to meet you, Jameson." She was gracious enough to ignore all my ridiculous ramblings and fluid spraying. "Looks like you ride quite a bit, huh?"

Time to get this conversation back on the rails. I was competent enough to have a normal conversation, I was sure of it. And I had an experiment to complete. "Why yes. I ride all the time. I find it helps keep me in shape and there's nothing quite like staying physically fit, you know?"

Her eyebrows rose up on her forehead. "Oh, for sure. I feel the same way." She lifted her arm and flexed her bicep muscle, none of which I could see because of the little white sweater she was wearing over her blouse.

"You, uh, lived here long?" I had to keep her talking. I wanted her to feel comfortable around me, not only for my experiment, but because we were now neighbors.

Her hand spun the wheel of my bike absentmindedly. Somewhere in my chest there was an odd tugging sensation. I liked her touching my things.

"Yep, I've lived in this house almost my whole life. It was my parents' house and they gave it to me when they moved to Arizona to retire about seven years ago. Now I'm raising my kids here." Her eyes went soft and I noticed their slate blue color.

"Wow, that's pretty amazing. Most people move more often than that around here. My son, Stein, and I moved in last weekend so I could start a new job. Before that, though, we've lived a couple other places already."

She nodded. "Yeah, I guess it is a bit weird to still be in the same house, but I love it. Lots of history." Her shoulders lifted and fell. "So, a new job, huh? What do you do for a living?"

"I'm a science professor at Pacific Coast College. You?" I shifted jerkily and my cleats scraped across the cement. *Damn shoes.*

Lily-Marie crossed her arms across her chest. "I work as an executive assistant at Disney."

That got my attention. "That's pretty cool. My son would love to hear that. He had a year or two where he was obsessed with *Cars*. Now he's too cool for any of that, but..." I shrugged.

"I hear you. My son, Clark, is eight. Said he met your son at school this week. He and my daughter, Mildred, are with their father this weekend, but we'll swing by and formally introduce ourselves soon."

I nodded. "That would be good." I could continue my experiment. "I'd love to help Stein make friends. Might also help ease the guilt of moving my kid to a new school."

She tapped the wheel of my bike. "Okay, well, have a nice ride. I'll, ah, see you soon."

I nodded again. "Yeah, sounds good. Have a good day."

Jesus Christ, how many times could I offer a lukewarm "good" in my sentence? "Good" was like the carrot shreds in a salad. It was simply there, but had no purpose. No one actually wanted to eat carrot in their salad. No one said "you know what's missing in this salad? What would really take the taste up a notch? Carrot shreds!" I wanted to be a deep-fried habanero pepper on top of her salad, not a limp shred of carrot to be pushed aside and forgotten.

She gave one last broad smile and then spun around and walked back to her house. When she got to the porch, she spun back around and caught me staring at her, trying to figure out how to be a different vegetable.

"Can I ask you for a favor?"

All thoughts of salads and word choices fled, leaving behind a renewed sense of confidence.

It's working! She's already reacting to my athleticism. These shorts must really accentuate my butt.

"Sure, what's up?" I took shallow breaths and remained calm.

She started wringing her hands and I was perplexed. It must be something really meaningful for her to find it difficult to even ask. Maybe she wanted to compliment me on my obvious athlete's body. Maybe she wanted to ask me out already, but didn't want to appear too forward. God bless Granny and her impeccable list.

Lily-Marie took a deep breath, dropped her hands, and thrust back her shoulders. My gaze wavered and dipped to the curves now thrust between us, but I wrangled it back up to her face in time for her question.

"Do you think we could help each other out with school drop-offs and pick-ups sometimes?" She rushed on. "I mean, our kids are at the same school every day, so it might make sense to carpool, you know?"

My amorous hopes were dashed, but I kept a smile in place. "Sure, sure. That makes sense. Why don't we introduce our kids and then see what makes sense?"

She blasted me with a mega-watt smile again and I felt taller just for having put that smile there. "Okay, sounds great! See you soon!" And then she bolted into her house.

I stood there lubing my chain, trying to figure out what just happened. My athleticism hadn't seemed to have any kind of effect on her, other than to get an introduction and a promise to share rides with our kids. Like neighbors. Or, at most, friends. Definitely not love.

Which was exactly in line with my hypothesis.

So why did I feel so let down?

I should be feeling relieved to have the first confirmation of my hypothesis. As I scanned my body, I noticed my chest felt heavy, my stomach was in knots, and joy was nowhere to be found. What was going on here?

I needed to get my eye on the prize and stop thinking about her eyelashes, so long they nearly hit her eyebrows. Or the way her body moved with the grace of a dancer, but the curves of Marilyn Monroe. I hadn't accounted for such beauty in my specimen for this experiment, but I wasn't a green scientist. I wouldn't be swayed from my goal.

Number two on the list was going down as a dud in the love column. Score one for my hypothesis. Nineteen more ways to try before proving my theory correct.

And in the meantime, I was going to ride thirty miles to burn the memory of her perfume out of my brain.

ily-Marie

"Get your ass over here."

Sunday morning dawned bright and beautiful, like most mornings in Southern California. But this morning was particularly bright, probably because I had a solid plan for starting on my list to find a husband. Today was pie-baking day.

I was on the phone with Gabby—who wasn't super supportive of my new man-magnet idea, I must confess. I'd explained everything to her yesterday and judging by the snorts and chuckles, she thought the whole thing was comical. I wouldn't let her negativity get me down, though. I'd take comical over getting pickpocketed again. No, thanks.

Her groan was the only answer.

"Seriously, Gabby. I need your help making these apple pies and the cookies for my new neighbor. Losing weight is on the list too, so I need you here to slap my hand if I try to eat the baked goods."

"What am I, the food police?"

"Yes! Now get over here and help me!"

I hung up on her and went to change out of my pajamas. After my run-in with Jameson yesterday, I wasn't going to be caught lounging in my pajamas all day like a total slouch. It got me hot and bothered and confused just thinking about him.

The man was hot, let me tell you. Dark, thick hair that had just a touch of wave to the longer bits on top. Tanned skin, even in January. And the bike shorts! Holy mother of pearl, those things were skin-tight and didn't hold back. I could see the outline of...well, everything. And, girl, I was *intrigued* with the size of his everything.

My ex, Shawn, had been good-looking, but he wasn't super muscular. In tighty-whities he looked a little ridiculous with his chicken legs, I'll be honest. But Jameson? Whoa, Nelly. Those legs were gorgeous and thick and muscular, especially encased in spandex. I'd wanted to climb his tree trunk legs and lay my head on his broad chest while my hands sank into his hair and held on tight for the ride.

On his bicycle. Duh.

He'd looked damn good, okay? But then he'd been super awkward, which was funny and a little bit charming. If nothing else, I was happy to have found another parent to carpool with when necessary. Hopefully the boys got along or I'd have to care-fully extricate myself from the arrangement.

I had a firm rule against shitting in the sand box where I played. That was a really gross analogy for not getting mixed up romantically with a neighbor. When I came home, those four walls were my sanctuary. My place to relax. I didn't want to have to pull the curtains, kill the lights, and dodge a romantic suitor gone wrong on my own sanctuary turf. Which meant putting

Jameson and his thighs of wonder out of my head and getting my bake on.

I finally had all the ingredients I had on hand laid out on the counter. I'd been thinking about Jameson the whole time I was getting ready to make my man-catching pies. Some might take that as a sign, but not me. I was in this to win Prince Charming and I was pretty sure a ripped, bicycle-loving, slacks-wearing science nerd was not him. While Jameson could sweep me off my feet literally, I highly doubted he possessed the characteristics to do it figuratively. So man-pies it was.

"I'm here, woman!" Gabby let herself in the front door, as usual. Once you've known someone for thirty years you give them free rein to come and go as they please.

I clapped my hands. "Excellent. Now we need to go to the store. I made a list."

Gabby rolled her eyes. "Of course you did. I assume you put coffee on that list for your bestie?"

I nodded graciously. "We can make a coffee run on the way back."

With that, we were on our way to the grocery store, no Jameson sighting, thank God. I filled Gabby in on the conversation yesterday, leaving out his physical attributes. She'd see him soon enough and I didn't want her teasing me about my hot-but-weird neighbor. If I didn't watch her closely, she would be setting me up on a date with every eligible man we encountered. Trust me, it had happened before.

We pulled into Vons and I grabbed my cloth grocery bag from the trunk before we crossed the parking lot and grabbed a cart. An old lady cut right in front of me, stealing the only cart in the carousel. How she managed it moving at a snail's pace, was beyond me, but the evidence was there. She rolled off into the store, smug smile and pokey pace her elderly version of the middle finger.

While counting to ten and walking to grab an empty cart off to the side of the store, I remembered my abbreviated list of Fifty Ways. Number three clearly stated to be nice to everyone as they may have an eligible son, father, brother, uncle who could ride off into the proverbial sunset with me. So instead of being passive aggressive and mumbling under my breath about her rude behavior or "accidentally" ramming my cart into hers as I entered the store, which I'd been known to do in the past, I pasted on a smile and called out a jaunty, "Good morning to ya!" as I passed her.

Gabby looked at me in horror. "What the hell's wrong with you? Are you feverish?" Her cold fingers probed my forehead as I tried to swat them away and still handle the shopping cart. "I've seen you verbally cut down lil' old grannies who just looked at you wrong at the grocery store before. You're kind of infamous with your old lady kerfuffles at the store."

"I'm fine. I'm just following my list. 'Be nice to everyone.'" I found the baking aisle and turned down the lane, scanning for white sugar and flour, hoping my blood pressure would get the message and calm down.

Gabby snorted and grabbed a box of sugar. "I'm telling you. This list is going to be downright comical. I won't even get into how sexist some of those items are on the original list. It's like sitting in a car watching a train wreck happen right in front of you. You want to look away, but you just can't miss all the gory details of the disaster, you know?"

I finally relinquished the cart to jab my fists onto my hips and narrow my eyes. "Thank you so much, bestie, for your vote of confidence. It really means the world to me that you're motivating me to find my happily ever after." The sarcasm was so tangy I'd need another box of sugar to cut it down.

Gabby looked unconcerned by my anger. "Careful. I might have a brother or uncle. Better be nice to me..."

The narrowed eyes turned into a full-on glacial death glare.

"I'm rethinking sharing everything with you. Clearly, I need to put a filter on my mouth. You can't be trusted."

She broke out into a smile and put her arm around my shoulders. I remained stiff as a board. "Ah, come on, Lil. I'm just teasing. You know you love me."

I shrugged her arm off and grabbed a bag of flour. "Yeah, yeah. Come on. Let's get out of here so I can make my man-pies."

Gabby followed me toward the checkout stands. "I'm not even going to comment on what those are. See? Totally supportive."

My eye roll was thwarted by the sight of the little old lady with her infamous cart holding exactly two items: a loaf of bread and a pack of gum. Perhaps the cart was just a substitute for a walker. Besides the utter emptiness of her cart, what *really* froze my eyeballs was the man walking next to her. He appeared shorter than my son and as bald as my daughter when she was first born. She smacked him in his belly with the back of her age-spotted hand when he tried to rush her to unload her two items onto the conveyer belt.

A tingling sensation crept over my skull. It may have been embarrassment or shame, I wasn't quite sure. Maybe it was just the sudden realization in real terms that my list of ways to get a husband might be as silly and unfruitful as Gabby thought it to be.

"You were so right," Gabby whispered in my ear. "You should totally get his number now that you were nice to her."

"Shut. Up."

She nudged me in the kidney with her elbow. "Seriously, bald guys are hot, didn't you know?"

I eyed the man in front of me, now trying to get dear old mom to push her cart through the checkout stand and collect her items on the other end. His pants were at least three inches above the back of his orthopedic black tennis shoes. And Gabby was wrong. He wasn't bald. He had two long, curly black hairs that originated on the back of his head and were combed to the side with the help of a generous glop of gel.

I swallowed hard and put my groceries on the belt, unable to look away from the old lady smacking her son with a grocery bag when he was too slow in bagging her stuff.

"I need you to shut up right now," I whispered savagely out of the side of my mouth.

Choked laughter fanned the flames of my embarrassment.

"You know, number twenty on my list is to make and sell toupees because bald guys are easy catches. Just be glad I had the sudden insight to nix that from my to-do list."

Gabby whooped out a loud laugh, turning the head of the old lady and earning us a frown. I just smiled serenely and waited for them to move along. Clearly, not *all* the things on the list were going to work for everyone. Hopefully the pies gave a better result than being nice.

Back at home, with coffee in hand, Gabby and I got busy rolling out dough and slicing apples. I tried three different ways to steer the conversation to Gabby's boyfriend, Hewitt, but she was avoiding my obvious traps and moved the talk to something far less personal. I was now officially worried about what was going on with them, but I knew Gabby would talk to me about it when she was ready. And today was not that day.

"Oh, crap."

Gabby spun around, rolling pin in hand. "What?"

I bit my thumbnail. "I forgot cinnamon."

"Who doesn't have cinnamon?" Gabby teased me.

"A mom whose kids hate oatmeal, that's who." I sighed and went to grab my purse by the door. "Back to the store I go."

"Why don't you just ask to borrow some from Mrs. Reynolds next door?"

Gabby was the voice of reason among the two of us. "That's a great idea. I'll be back in a flash."

I dropped my purse, jammed my feet into my ratty slippers,

and rushed over to Mrs. Reynolds' house. I rang the doorbell and hopped from foot to foot to keep warm. After a significant wait and a second jab to the doorbell, I had to face the fact that no one was home. I spun around to traipse back across the lawn and grab my purse for the trip to the store after all when my gaze landed on Jameson's house.

What were the odds he'd have cinnamon on hand?

What were the odds he'd be in skin-tight biker shorts again?

I hustled across my lawn and up to his door, taking a deep breath before ringing his doorbell. I was there for cinnamon, not a peek at his muscles. Besides, it would take having all my wits about me to navigate a conversation with him, as awkward as he was.

The door swung open and there he stood, creased slacks, dark blue sweater vest over a button-down shirt, and a severe expression. His thick eyebrows were drawn, a significant valley gouging between his eyes.

"Um, hi! Sorry to disturb you." I went for a smile, but he continued to look at me with that expression. His eyes had a hazy look to them, like he was seeing me, but not really seeing me. It made about as much sense as my previous interaction with him. I forged ahead. My man-pies were desperate. "Okay, so, I'm baking some apple pies and just realized I forgot to buy cinnamon. Any chance you have some lying around I could use?"

He stared at me for a beat longer before his eyebrows relented and his gaze cleared. "Uh, sure. I think I have some. Come on in." He backed away from the door and spun on his heel—yes, he was wearing dress shoes in his own house—and walked toward a doorway that I presumed led to the kitchen. I shuffled behind in my fuzzy slippers.

"All our stuff is still kind of packed away, but I'm sure I can find it." He came to an abrupt stop and I almost ran into his broad back, my slippers giving very little traction on the wood floor.

I backed off quickly and silently, and peered around him. There were three large open cardboard boxes in the middle of his kitchen. One was packed to the top with small appliances and all manner of spatulas and serving spoons. Another held a year's supply of canned soup. The last one was a mystery in that everything in it was wrapped in brown packing paper.

He stood there staring at the three boxes, not moving.

"So, you guys like soup?" I could have slapped my forehead. What the hell kind of question was that? Felt like the awkward conversation virus was spreading and I was its current victim.

He whipped his head toward me, like he'd forgotten I was there. "Oh, yeah. I'm not much of a cook, so I keep a lot of soup on hand. Pretty hard to mess that up."

Then he started digging around in the small appliance box, setting a lemon pepper container on the counter, then a garlic salt shaker, before finally unearthing the cinnamon container from under the toaster.

"Aha! I knew I had it." He presented it to me like a proud cat dragging in a dead mouse.

"Well, thanks. You've saved me a trip to the store. I appreciate it. I'll bring it back shortly." I hugged the bottle to my chest and inched my way out of the kitchen.

He waved off my suggestion. "No worries. Take your time. I rarely use cinnamon." Then he grinned and I froze for a second. Gone was the nerdy professor, in its place a handsome man who could turn female heads if he only tried. Then he frowned and I could breathe again. I must have been mistaken, the glimpse too brief to have been real.

"Okay, well, thanks again." I lifted the cinnamon in some sort of weird toast and then hightailed it back to the front door. I had to get out of there. I barely knew the man. I probably shouldn't have come in his house what with all the crazy stories you heard about murders and kidnappings in Southern California.

I was halfway to my house when I heard his front door finally click shut.

"Hey, Mrs. Reynolds came through, huh?" Gabby smiled at the cinnamon in my hand when I came into the kitchen.

"Not really. I got this from my new neighbor, Jameson." I got busy finding the teaspoons to measure it into the apple and sugar mixture.

"Jameson, huh? He sounds hot." Gabby elbowed me. "Is he?"

I didn't meet her eyes, just kept mixing the apples so they were thoroughly coated with the cinnamon and sugar. These pies had to be perfect so Mr. Future Lily-Marie would know how fabulous I was and want to taste all my other delightful desserts, if you know what I mean.

"Um, not really. He's kind of a nerdy professor, to be honest."

"Hmm...sometimes those types are actually the really hot ones under their glasses. Looks can be deceiving, you know?"

"He doesn't wear glasses, I don't think. Sweaters, yes. But not glasses."

Gabby was staring at the side of my head. I could feel her stare, but I refused to take the bait. If I showed any type of interest she'd be marching next door to rope Jameson into a date with me. Nope. Not gonna happen. I had my own plan.

The doorbell rang out and we both jumped.

"I'll get it." I was all too happy to escape the kitchen and Gabby's hawk-like attention.

I swung open the door to find Jameson standing there, his frown gone, thankfully. It was replaced by a smudge of dirt on his cheek. My hand lifted a few inches before I realized what I was doing and forced it back down to my side. His dirt smudge was none of my business and my fingers certainly did not need to swipe it away.

"Hi." He waved from two feet away. "I found something else I thought you might need for your apple pies."

He handed me a blue and white ceramic pie cutter, clearly

older than both of us. It looked like an antique, charming and yet still useful so many decades later.

"It was my grandmother's." He shrugged.

"Oh. Thanks. I actually could use that." I hooked a thumb over my shoulder. "I'm taking these pies to work tomorrow. All the single guys there devour desserts, so I'll have to show them how to slow down and cut a proper piece." I laughed, but he didn't join in. Instead, the frown was back full force, the eyebrows nearly puckered into a unibrow.

He didn't answer, so after a beat or two I tried to fill the silence. "So, how about I have you and your son over sometime this week so our kids can meet?"

He nodded, a quick jerk of the head, no warmth in the movement whatsoever. "Sure."

"Okay. How about Wednesday?"

Another head jerk. "Wednesday it is."

I smiled and slowly closed the door while he just stood there. When the door was finally closed, I grimaced from yet another ungainly conversation.

"Who was that?" Gabby joined me, peeking out the front window like the nosey woman she is.

"Never mind." I headed back to the kitchen, needing to divert her as quickly as possible.

Those two could never meet.

6

ameson

"I probably could have handled that better."

I was mumbling to myself as I got ready for our dinner over at Lily-Marie's house on Wednesday night. Nodding to myself in the full-length mirror, I eyed the new jeans I'd bought for the occasion, feeling like my reflection was a stranger. I couldn't remember the last time I wore jeans or had an easygoing conversation with a woman.

As soon as Lily-Marie shut the door in my face on Sunday, I'd gone back to my house and berated myself for my lack of social skills. I'd been elbow deep into my lecture planning for microbiology when she rang my doorbell. I'd gone from fungal pathogenesis to staring at Lily-Marie's beautiful face, her long hair up in a bun with strands escaping to frame her face perfectly. Could anyone blame me for stuttering and stammering like a mute middle schooler in the presence of a blond angel?

By the time I'd reengaged my brain, she was gone, off to bake pies at her place. The list specifically said not to be a bookworm and I'd failed that task miserably. Then I remembered another item on the list and how it encouraged men to do nice things. Unexpected things. So I dug through my kitchen boxes until I found my grandmother's pie cutter I'd never had the occasion to use but still schlepped around from house to house. It was time to redeem myself.

That second conversation should have gone so much better. I was prepared with my nice gesture and I'd gotten out all my awkwardness in the first conversation. I even remembered to lead with a smile. But then she'd said something about single men at work eating her pies and my brain had taken the ride with my stomach when it dropped down to my feet. I didn't want these coworkers eating her pie or anything else. *I* wanted her pie.

Or, I wanted her to at least offer me her pie. I didn't even really like pie, but the offer would have been nice. You know. For the sake of my experiment.

My grandmother had written her list of fifty ways with a more natural conversationalist in mind, I was sure. It wasn't her fault the list wasn't working; it was mine. And tonight was my opportunity to get it right. I owed it to the entire field of science to really give this experiment a fair try. My bumbling beginnings could be smoothed over as quickly as tonight when we had dinner at her place.

I had on my favorite forest green sweater over a tan striped collared shirt. My hair was actually cooperating and my shoes had undergone a fresh buffing that morning. I even dug out my trusty bottle of cologne from a box of toiletries I hadn't gotten around to unpacking yet. I said trusty, but I didn't know that I'd ever relied on it to do anything more than make me smell like an Abercrombie model. I didn't look like one, but maybe I could smell like one and, as such, catch the olfactory senses of a beautiful lady. From there, it was up to my conversational skills to keep her head turned my way. And those were definitely *not* trusty.

"Dad!" Stein skidded into my room, his socks sliding along the wooden floor. "Can I wear my favorite T-shirt?"

I loved that boy with all my heart, but he had zero fashion sense. Which, coming from me, said quite a bit. His favorite T-shirt was from three years and ten growth spurts ago. It was snug, to say the least, causing his arms to jut out at a ninety-degree angle from his body.

Tilting my head, I tried to come up with placating words that wouldn't send him stomping to his room with hurt feelings while I also wondered why that shirt hadn't gotten "lost" in the move. That had been the fate of a few other items and I was disappointed in myself that I'd missed that one.

"When meeting new friends for the first time, you should always put your best foot forward. Now, that is a really nice shirt, but something a little newer might be a better choice for tonight." There. That was nice.

His little face scrunched up. "Why does it matter what shirt I wear if it's my foot I'm forwarding? Do you mean shoes, Dad?"

I resisted the urge to run my hands through my hair. My new wax pomade was not designed for fathers of eight-year-old boys. "Get a new shirt on, buddy. How about that blue one we bought the other day?"

He rolled his eyes and ran out the bedroom door, hopefully able to get out of that old shirt before it started restricting blood flow. By the time I finished rolling my pants and sweater with a lint roller, Stein was back, the blue polo shirt over his jeans.

"Ready?"

He gave me a head nod, and while he might have been ready to go to dinner, I could tell he wasn't ready to talk to me. He always went silent when he was mad at me. I thought of my list again and remembered the one about well-behaved children and refraining from yelling at them in front of the ladies. I wasn't a yeller anyway, but considering how badly I was messing everything else up, I'd better cover all my bases.

I walked to the front door and Stein followed behind me. Before I opened it, I crouched down and tugged him to me.

"We're meeting new friends, so let's be on our best behavior, all right?"

His gray eyes stared back at me with so much trust, I wanted to freeze time and hug him to my chest for all eternity. That piercing ache in my chest? That was love. But from my experience, and those in my circle, that kind of love was not possible in a romantic way. It was puppy-dog eyes and holding hands and being obnoxiously cute in public, but it wasn't an arrow straight through the chest that you'd gladly live with for the rest of your life if you could only get to love that someone. Romantic love wasn't truly love at all. At best, it was affection.

"Oh! I almost forgot." I ran into the kitchen and grabbed the bouquet of flowers I'd kept in a vase of water since I got home from my last class of the day. Bright yellow sunflowers with pink roses and white baby's breath. They'd reminded me of Lily-Marie when I saw them, so I went with it.

"Let's do this, Stein-man." I held out my fist, which he bumped with his small one, and off we marched next door.

I lifted my hand to knock on the door, but it swung open, revealing Lily-Marie's daughter.

"Hello. You must be Mr. MacMill and Stein." Her blond curls were a messy halo around her head. Even as we heard Lily-Marie call her from the back of the house, reminding her not to open the door, her gap-tooth smile stayed in place. She shrugged her little shoulders and I struggled to hold in my chuckle.

"Milly, you know better than to answer the door without me." Lily-Marie walked up to the door and I nearly squashed the flowers before I remembered to lighten my grip. "Welcome, gentlemen." Her smile lit up, its wattage matching the bright yellow dress she had on.

Without taking my eyes off her face, I pushed Stein forward and entered the house behind him. I thrust the flowers in the space between us, a strange quaking beginning in my torso region when her eyes lit up at the offering.

She put her hands on the bouquet, her pinkie brushing against mine. "Thank you so much for the flowers. They're beautiful!" Another dazzling smile and then she was whirling around, taking the flowers and my attention into the kitchen.

"Dad?" Stein tugged on my arm and I turned with a start, remembering the kids were in the room too. "Mind if I go out back and play with Clark?"

I nodded quickly and smiled absentmindedly, my gaze split between him and Lily-Marie's backside. "Sure, sure. Go have fun, son."

He ran out of the room with Clark, Milly following behind, an energetic ball of short limbs trying to move fast enough to keep up with the boys. I followed Lily-Marie into the kitchen to find her scrounging around a bottom cabinet, her pretty dress brushing against the floor. Moving quickly to her side, I squatted down and offered assistance.

"Here, let me help you."

She pulled her head out of the cabinet, her cheeks flushed pink. "Thanks. I know I have a vase in here somewhere."

I leaned in closer to get a better view of the dimly lit space, ever conscious of her body just inches away from mine. If I leaned just a bit to the right, I'd be close enough to kiss her.

Not that I had any intention of doing that.

Just that I could have. If I'd wanted to. Which I didn't.

My sweater suddenly seemed like a bad choice as it was a million degrees in this house. No wonder she was blushing. We were in danger of heatstroke.

Before I could pass out from dehydration, I spotted a sparkling crystal vase in the back of the cabinet. I reached as far in as my long arms would allow and scooped it out, handing it to her and standing up.

I swayed for a second, thinking I just might pass out after all. Black dots swam in my vision and I gripped the counter to stay upright. The collar of my shirt was restricting air flow, so I gave it a stiff tug and blinked my eyes. The dots went away as I focused on Lily-Marie filling the vase with water and arranging the flowers, her back to me.

"These are just gorgeous. You know it's funny, I'm so used to people getting me lilies that I've come to hate them." She glanced over her shoulder at me, that smile just as dazzling as the first time I saw it.

I shook my head, confused. "Why would everyone get you lilies?"

Her smile froze. She set the flowers down and spun around, crossing her arms over her chest. "Jameson MacMillan. What is my name?"

I scrunched up my face, unsure why I was in trouble. "Lily-Mar—oh, I get it." Jesus H. Christ, I needed to get my act together. She would think I was some sort of dimwit when the reality was that her smile short-circuited my brain every single time.

Before she could laugh at me like I deserved, I took a deep breath and infused some cheerfulness into my voice that I didn't actually feel. "So, can I help you make anything?"

She opened the fridge and pulled out a platter of steaks. "Nope. I have a salad all ready to go, bread rolls in the oven, and I just need to put these on the grill." She tilted her head to the counter across from me. "Maybe you can open the wine and pour us a glass?"

That I could handle way better than conversation. I nodded and she walked out with the steaks. I grabbed the bottle of red wine, seeing it was a cab from a little winery in Sonoma. That weird quaking in my belly was back when I realized she hadn't gone cheap with the wine nor the food for our little dinner. I wasn't sure what that meant, but I just hoped the feeling wasn't indigestion or gas. That was the last thing I needed.

I poured the wine and set our glasses on the table, then went to round up the kids and have them wash their hands. I was pleased to see that Clark and Milly were well-behaved kids, not even making faces when I made them use soap. It only took one peek at germs in a microscope to make you more conscious of hygiene.

"I hope you're hungry, kiddos!" Lily-Marie came through the kitchen, grabbed the salad out of the fridge, and pulled the rolls out of the oven to put them in a bread basket.

The kids ran to the table and had a seat. I gave Lily-Marie a smile, taking the bread basket from her, and followed her, sitting down only after she sank into one of the chairs at the head of the table. I gazed at her smiling face across the table and lost the grin as something shifted. Something inside me. Like a bubble of gas maybe.

"You okay, Jameson?" Lily-Marie was staring at me with concern while the kids were busy buttering their rolls and flinging salad onto their plates.

"Oh, yes, fine." I picked up the platter of steaks and selected a thick one. "These look great." I passed the plate to Stein and told him to pass it to Lily-Marie.

Whatever was going on with my digestive system would have to wait. I'd eat every bite on my plate just so Lily-Marie knew I appreciated all the work she put into making this homemade meal. It was a rarity for Stein and me to go to this much trouble since it was just the two of us. I'm sure he was marveling at the food too.

When I saw Lily-Marie had all her food on her plate and had taken the first bite of salad, I picked up my knife and cut a piece of steak. It looked pretty pink for an outside piece, but then again, I was more of a well-done steak kind of guy anyway.

A few more bites in and I wasn't sure if I could keep going.

The fluttering was back, but it was more of a gagging sensation. The center of the steak was so red I could have sworn it still had a heartbeat. With a strong swallow and an iron will, not to mention stomach, I moved on to the salad, pushing it to the far side of my plate to miss the puddle of red seeping out from under my steak.

"So, Stein, what sports do you play?" Lily-Marie was politely engaging my son in conversation, which helped draw my focus from the carnage on my plate.

My chest swelled with pride when Stein swallowed before answering. "I play soccer right now, but I kinda want to try baseball."

"Hey, I play baseball. You wanna play catch with me later? I can show you how." Clark interjected, his big blue eyes sparkling at the thought of a new buddy to play with.

"I pway too!" Milly nearly jumped out of her chair to climb the table and get in on the fun.

"Let's let the boys get some baseball time in and then I'm sure they'll let you play some catch too." Lily-Marie successfully refereed what looked like a common issue between the two siblings. She gave me a wink and I nearly choked on the leafy greens.

"Oh, I forgot the ketchup. My heathens like it on their steak." She hopped up and I stood abruptly too, nearly tipping my chair over in the process. She gave me a funny look, but ran into the kitchen anyway. My list said to stand whenever a woman stood. I believed it was to show respect, quite like opening doors for women, but I wasn't sure if she would take it that way.

When she came back in, I waited for her to sit, and then took my seat as well, smoothing my napkin back over my lap.

"So, what specifically do you do for Disney?" I figured showing interest in Lily-Marie's line of work would have been on Granny's list had she made the list in more modern times.

She chewed a bite of steak and then answered. "I'm an admin for one of the marketing executives, so it's a little bit of everything, to be honest. I've learned so much in this position. It's an incredible company."

She cut another section of steak and took a bite as Stein asked her a question. "Do they give you free Disney DVDs?"

She quit chewing and her face took on a paler shade. She put a napkin up to her mouth and coughed. When she pulled it away, she finally answered. "Um, yes. We do. We get a lot of the movies for our personal collection and when they have special editions. One of the many perks."

I decided I'd better work on a roll, rather than attempt the steak again. "What's everyone's favorite Disney movie?" I asked the table.

"Ohhh, I wuv Cindy-wella." Milly smiled a cheesy grin, one I couldn't help but return. Damn, that kid was cute.

"I used to love *Cars*, so I'd say that's still my favorite," Stein answered, with Clark nodding his agreement.

Lily-Marie put another bite of steak in her mouth, then promptly spat it back out onto her plate. Everyone stared at her and her bad table manners.

She looked up, eyes wide and face heated. "I'm so sorry. Oh my goodness. It's just the steak is way too rare."

I shrugged. "Yeah, it's a little on the rare side, but still good," I reassured her.

"It's still cold in the middle," she confessed.

"Yeah," I agreed with a grimace, then burst out laughing.

She stared at me for a second and then began laughing too. "Oh my God. It's so bad! Why didn't you say something?"

"You went to a lot of trouble and I really appreciate it. No reason to complain." I held out my hand across the table. "In fact, let me have your plate. I can put it back on the grill."

"No, no. I've got it." Lily-Marie stood up, which of course, meant I had to stand up too. She cocked her head to the side, but took my plate without a word. We discussed movies until she came back, well-done steaks still sizzling from the grill.

She sat down and took one bite before jumping up again. I stood for a third time, wondering if I should have stretched before coming over, not realizing I'd be getting a squat workout with my dinner. She gave me a look I couldn't decipher and then sat down again without going to the kitchen. I narrowed my eyes at her and sat back down to eat the rest of my dinner without further interruption.

By the time we finished dessert, Milly was lying in Lily-Marie's lap, completely asleep. The boys had to be rounded up and forced to quit playing. After a million "thank yous" for the dinner and conversation, we left for the long walk home.

"Whatcha smiling about, Dad?" Stein asked through a yawn as I unlocked our front door.

"Just thinking about a science experiment of mine," I replied.

The most fun one I'd ever been a part of.

ily-Marie

"I think one of the kids stole my headphones again."

I had my cell phone wedged between my ear and my shoulder, probably giving myself a crick in the neck that wouldn't go away for days, but I couldn't wait to talk to Gabby. She'd been crazy busy the whole week and I hadn't gotten to download her on how my man-pies went over with the single guys at work, or how dinner went with Jameson a few days ago.

But my hands were required elsewhere when a sewing needle was jabbing up and down in a rapid fire staccato on the herringbone twill that would soon be my new skirt. I was a mother, therefore, a master multitasker.

"You need to get a Bluetooth headset. They wouldn't steal those." When I snorted—because hello, have you seen how expensive those are—she continued. "Just put me on speakerphone."

"Okay, but the kids are upstairs watching a movie, so keep the f-bombs on lockdown, sailor."

"Yeah, yeah. What's all the racket anyway?"

I took my foot off the pedal on the floor and straightened my back. I'd been hunched over the ancient sewing machine for thirty minutes already. My mom taught me how to sew when I was a little girl, on this same machine in fact, but it never held my interest back then. Plus, with how expensive fabric was these days it proved cheaper and easier to just buy the clothes from a store.

"I'm making a skirt." I adjusted the material to start sewing the hem along the bottom.

There was a long pause. "Like, with a hot glue gun? Or staples or something?"

I shook my head, which is quite a talent while still holding a cell phone between one's head and shoulder. "Seriously? Who makes a skirt with a hot glue gun?"

"Well, excuse me. You take up some crazy new hobby and I'm supposed to just know? Gonna make your shoes too now? Maybe get a horse and ride that to work?"

Now the pause was on my end. "Wow. Someone is grumpy. Hew not giving you what you need?"

"Hey, keep Hew out of this. What's with the skirt, Martha Stewart?"

"Well, according to my list, I need to make something myself and wear it. Men derive some high level of primal satisfaction in knowing a woman can do these sorts of crafts."

I heard a loud snort from the other end. "You know you're single-handedly setting back the women's movement by at least half a decade, right? I mean, what are you going to do next? Give up your right to vote so you don't threaten the intelligence level of the male species?"

Pressing my foot onto the pedal and feeding the material through the machine slowly, I responded, "Calm down, gender inequality freedom fighter. I'm just making a skirt, not fetching 'the man' his slippers. Now put the filter on, I'm putting you on speaker." I stopped the sewing machine to put the phone down on the table next to me. Not a moment too soon either, as my neck started to spasm. "It's hard to believe, but I didn't call you to discuss the unfair division of labor. I gotta tell you about my pies!"

Gabby laughed, sounding like my best friend for the first time this phone call. "You know, I really should stop giving you a hard time about this plan. It's turning out to provide a ridiculous amount of entertainment for me. If you're happy, I'm happy. Now spill. Did the apple pie give you any *American Pie* moments?"

I fed more material through the machine, biting my lip in concentration. "You know that makes us sound really old when you reference movies from twenty years ago, right?"

"Get to the good stuff," Gabby deadpanned.

I rolled my eyes, which is never a good idea around a sharp needle. "I'm not sure how much good stuff there really is. I brought my pies to work and they brought all the boys to the yard, but they were so busy stuffing their faces, I barely got to talk to them. I went around the room checking out their ring finger, and if it was bare, I was on 'em like white on rice. I got a lot of 'thank yous' and pats on the back, but no phone numbers. You know how in marketing they say it takes seven touches before people take notice of something?"

"Um, yeah?"

"Well, I got to thinking that maybe I need to repeat my pie offering a few more times to really get their attention."

"Or maybe—and this is radical, so hold on to your skirt—you should drop the man-pies idea and move on to another thing on your list. I think it's safe to say that tactic didn't work. I'd hate to see you turn your kitchen into a bakery when it's not netting you any actual men."

Starting the sewing machine back up, I went super slow, adjusting as I went to keep the seam straight. Or straight-ish. "You might be right. I'll think on that, but that's not all I got. I had dinner with the new next-door neighbor Wednesday night and I tried out a new tactic."

"Mr. Tall, Dark, and Mysterious?"

"Yep, that's the one. He brought his son over, who totally clicked with Clark. He brought me flowers, but the conversation was a little awkward, like every interaction with him. But get this: I grilled steaks like the list said to do!"

"And? He got on one knee and asked for your hand?"

"No, smart-ass, I spat out a half-chewed piece onto my plate."

"What? Gross, Lil."

I giggled. "I know. It said to make the steaks rare, but I went a little overboard. Or under board. They were so raw it was freezing cold in the center! I wondered why Jameson had stopped eating his steak. Guess he likes his meat without a side of salmonella."

"A swing and a miss!" Gabby used some weird accent she swore sounded like Vin Scully, the legendary announcer for the Dodgers, but actually sounded like some East Coast mafia man from a made-for-television movie.

"Yeah, yeah. One of these days I'll find the thing on the list that works. Just you wait. I can feel it." I got to the end of the hem, tracing backward and forward before cutting off the thread and examining my work. "What was even funnier was Jameson's behavior."

"In what way? And wait a second. You haven't told me what he looks like yet. I only saw him from behind and from far away. Don't leave your bestie hangin'."

I squinted my eyes and pinned the zipper into the top of the skirt. This was dangerous territory, both in the conversation and in the sewing project. "Let's see. He's tall, got dark hair that he gels on top. Kind of reminds me of a 1940s debonair kind of guy. Probably uses some old-school pomade to get his hair like that. He's muscular, but not overly so. His eyes are like a non-color."

"He sounds delicious so far. But what the hell is a non-color?"

"I don't know exactly. It's like his eyes are straight gray. And I'll be honest, he's attractive in a classic kind of way, but every conversation with him has been awkward at best, so don't bark up that tree."

Gabby sighed. "Okay, fine. But I reserve the right to see for myself how eligible this neighbor might be. Tell me about this odd behavior."

Happy she was distracted from matchmaking, I started sewing the zipper into the skirt. "It started when I stood up to grab something from the kitchen. The second I stood up from the table, he stood up too. And stayed standing until I got back. And then when I hopped up to put the steaks back on the grill, he stood again. So a few minutes later I stood up for no reason just to test it out. And he stood up too! What's up with that?"

"Hmm. I don't know. That's definitely weird. I'll have to Google it and see if I can come up with—"

"Ouch!" I pulled my hand back and examined my fingertip. While sewing the zipper, I'd jabbed myself hard with one of the pins in the top of my middle finger. A drop of blood bubbled up and I took a deep breath to keep from freaking out.

"You okay?" I heard Gabby's voice calling to me from the phone, like she was down a long tunnel.

Most moms learn to deal with all manner of bodily fluids. I mean. You're a mom. You had to clean up diapers from day one with substances that were too ghastly to talk about. Kids ate a whole hot dog and then vomited all over you, chunks of half-digested pressed meat tangled in your hair. Shit happens. A lot.

So you'd think I'd be able to handle the sight of blood a lot better than half the population. Turns out blood was my kryptonite.

"Blood," I mumbled. "Call ya back."

I hung up on her and went into the kitchen for a paper towel. If I got the blood covered up I'd be fine. Once the paper towel was wound around my finger, I instantly started feeling better. A quick trip to the medicine cabinet in the downstairs bathroom and I got a Band-Aid on my finger without further wooziness.

"Crisis averted," I said out loud to the empty room.

"Did you say something, Mom?" Clark called down from upstairs, the movie blaring through the open door.

"I'm good! Just talking to myself again," I called up. The door closed and the movie muted. They were used to my crazy.

Cautiously, I went back to the sewing machine and finished the zipper. Figured I'd better try it on before I hand-sewed the button in place. Shimmying out of my jeans, I stepped into the skirt and pulled it up, pleased to see the hem length was perfect. Not too long like an old maid, but not so short my cellulite was showing. I had standards, okay?

I reached back and zipped it up, needing to suck in a little before it went all the way up. It was a bit tighter than I'd prefer, but the idea of letting out a seam seemed more daunting than sewing the damn thing in the first place. My sense of achievement dimmed until I remembered that part of my fifty ways was to go on a diet. If I did a little of that torture, my skirt actually might fit just fine.

The doorbell rang out, startling me. I wasn't expecting anyone, so I approached the door slowly and looked out the peephole. It was dirty and therefore hard to see out, considering I hadn't cleaned the peephole in—well, never. But even through a film of filth, it looked like Jameson on my doorstep.

I swung the door open and gave him a genuine smile. After our dinner, I decided I liked the guy. Yeah, he was awkward, but he was a nice person and our boys seemed to get along. And he was even a smidge good-looking underneath all those grandpa sweaters.

"Jameson! Come on in." I pulled back and let him pass, taking the moment to check out the crease in his slacks as he walked by. Damn, he must have an industrial strength iron.

He twirled around and flashed his teeth in an easy smile. He had a nice one. His expression could be on the harsh side most of the time, so when he smiled, it practically transformed his face.

"Sorry to drop in uninvited, but I thought we should hash out the carpool plan for the week ahead. I would have called, but then I realized I don't have your number." His gaze dropped and he shifted, leaning one shoulder against the wall, suddenly very invested as to what was in his pockets.

"Oh, yeah, that's a good idea." I walked ahead of him into the kitchenette area where my sewing machine was set up and where I'd left my cell phone. I could swear I felt his gaze traveling along the back of my bare legs. My cheeks flushed as I remembered I had on the skirt I was making. Probably looked a little weird with the T-shirt I had on.

His throat cleared behind me. "Is that, um, a new skirt? It looks lovely."

I grabbed my phone and spun around, flattered by his compliment but still uncomfortable in this weird outfit. My skirt wasn't ready for its debut into the world. I guess Jameson would be its trial run.

"Thanks. I just made it this afternoon. Still have some finishing things to do to it." I trailed off, out of breath now that I had to hold my stomach in with the tight material pressing into my belly.

"Wow. You made it yourself? That's impressive. I can't even make toast without burning it. I can't imagine making my own clothes." Jameson smiled warmly, and despite my doubts, I started to feel beautiful under his gaze.

"Thanks," I gushed again. Great, now I was repeating myself. I unlocked my phone and pulled up a new contact. "Okay, what's your number?"

He gave it to me and I called it so he had my number too. Something about giving him my phone number felt intimate. Maybe it was the compliment stacked on top of it. We were just parents working together to give rides to our kids, but it felt like there was more to getting my number than the carpool idea.

His face turned into a harsh frown and dashed my hope that he was wanting my number so he could call me. I was oddly unsettled, way too excited for even just a moment about this virtual stranger calling me.

"Did you hurt yourself?" He reached out and brushed his fingertips over the hand holding my phone. I felt the touch to the tips of my toes, but ignored that feeling to focus on the conversation.

"Yeah, just a pinprick from sewing." I shrugged like it was nothing, because it really was.

"Better get a new Band-Aid. Looks like it's bleeding through."

The blood drained from my head and I swayed as I stood there. "Really?"

He looked up at me, then back down at my finger. "Really." Then back up at me. "Are you okay?"

My eyes glazed over. "I really hate blood."

He straightened off the wall. "Tell me where the Band-Aids are. I'll change it out for you."

As much as that sounded like exactly what I needed, I couldn't let him deal with my bloody Band-Aid. That was just gross.

"Oh no, that's a kind offer, but I got it." I walked toward the bathroom, still not looking down at my finger. Even in my freaked-out haze, I could hear Jameson trailing behind me. It was more comforting than annoying to have him there to witness my ridiculousness. Like I could just sense that he'd take care of me if I let him.

When I reached the bathroom and pulled the Band-Aids out of the medicine cabinet, Jameson grabbed my hand, careful to stay away from the offending appendage. He slowly peeled off the Band-Aid and I instinctively looked away the moment I saw red. I should have pulled away and taken care of it myself, but there was something oddly addictive about someone taking care of me. He held my hand with such attentiveness I kept it there, mesmerized by his big hands engulfing mine.

I'd covered all manner of wounds with Band-Aids when my kids hurt themselves, all the while holding back my nausea and trying to get it over with as soon as possible. Not Jameson. He moved with precision, taking his time to get it right. His eyebrows pinched together as he examined my finger. Not only did he smooth a new Band-Aid in place, but he put a dot of ointment on the Band-Aid in case of infection. All without conversation. Just touch.

I suddenly felt guilty for all the times I'd hurriedly bandaged my kiddos and sent them off before I passed out. I wondered if they'd felt the care and attention I felt in this heady moment.

Like a lightbulb suddenly illuminating the conflicting emotions racing through my system, I realized the list was finally working! It said to wear a Band-Aid so the gentlemen ask you about it. Probably to drum up conversation, but to also evoke sympathy. Honestly, it sounded insane when I read it, but hot damn, it was the only thing that seemed to have worked so far. And boy, did it work.

Jameson cleared his throat again and stepped back, his hands dropping mine slowly. He straightened up and nodded quickly before spinning around and walking back to my living room. I took a deep breath and pressed my newly bandaged hand to my stomach before following him.

"Thank you. I really don't do so well with blood." My voice rang out loudly in the room, like even the walls were startled we were back to talking, not touching.

A small smile slid across his lips. "No problem at all."

So, here's a small detail about me that really only Gabby knows. When I get flustered, I also get a little weird. Like my brain short-circuits and I engage in all manner of weird acts with clearly no forethought. Like a newborn foal trying to walk for the first time, all limbs and jerky, uncoordinated movements. I explain all this so you understand my quirkiness and perhaps extend a little more forgiveness when I do stupid things.

Because I was flustered all right. This man had held my hand with such tenderness, I'd felt it in the pit of my stomach. And then add in the blood and my thoughts were jumbled. On top of this fluster sundae was the kernel of hope flaring to life that this list of fifty ways might actually glean results.

The list had also said dropping the handkerchief still worked. That was the only thought that flittered through my brain at that moment. So I did. Drop something, that is. And that's where some forethought would have been helpful. Dropping a handkerchief is an elegant move as it floats down to rest gently against the man's feet. Reaching out and grabbing the first thing within reach —my sewing scissors—is not so elegant, come to find out.

I threw those scissors down in what my addled brain thought looked like a careless mistake, but was in fact more of a dart-throwing motion. Jameson jumped back as any reasonable person would when a sharp object was being hurtled in their direction. The scissors, thankfully, flew to the ground without striking him, letting out a thunderous boom when they met with my wood floor. They lay there motionless, both of us staring at the scissors like we couldn't believe they were there and not on the table where they should have been.

My brain finally caught up to my body's actions and wanted to dig a deep hole and disappear. Considering I didn't have the callouses for that much shovel work, I considered—finally, some consideration—the option to pick up the scissors and go with the lie that it had been an accident. Jameson didn't make a move to pick them up, so clearly my list wasn't working again, so the only option was to feign ignorance.

"Oh my God, I'm so sorry. I didn't see them there." I leaped forward and bent down to pick them up. Just as my hand closed over the handle, my skirt decided to have no part of catching me a man. A loud ripping noise joined the weird sounds this room had endured all day, followed by a gust of cool air on my backside. The skirt that had once been too tight, now felt ridiculously loose.

I whipped up faster than my kids when they smelled bacon in the morning and shuffled backward, scissors clutched to my chest. My eyes were wide, staring at Jameson, gauging his reaction. I wondered if I was acting normally enough for him to let it go. It wasn't a good sign when my brain started laughing at me in my own head.

His eyes shifted from my face, to the scissors in my hands, then down to the rapidly falling skirt of mine, then back to my face. I saw a mix of emotions there that would have been comical on any other day if it had been happening to anyone else. When his gaze went through the cycle again, I saw concern when he looked at my face, fear when he took in the scissors, and a hunger when he traced the movement of my skirt shifting down my legs with each shuffle backward.

The final straw to the awkward stare-down happened when my skirt made a run for it and dropped down my legs entirely, leaving me there in my T-shirt and underwear.

And a blanket of humiliation.

ameson

The sun wasn't even up yet, but I was awake, enjoying the still moments under the warm covers before the morning hustle began. My alarm hadn't gone off yet, but my brain was up and firing, thinking about Lily-Marie. Not as a science experiment, but as a person. A friend.

A psycho.

A silent bubble of laughter rolled up from my chest. I hadn't even had coffee yet and a big smile was taking up residence on my face. The woman intrigued me more than I could say, but the truth was...she was a little scary.

She'd opened the door wearing the weirdest outfit and then practically passed out over a tiny nick on her finger. Then in thanks she hurled scissors at my feet, like they'd offended her with their size thirteen lace-up oxfords. To top it all off, her skirt kept sliding down and all she did was inch backward, her eyes locked to my face, like she was trying to hypnotize me into not noticing she was dropping her skirt.

Of course that attempt went out the window when her skirt hit the floor and I got a flash sighting of her pale legs and pink cotton underwear. I looked away of course—I wasn't an asshole—but the image was still locked in my brain, waiting for this exact moment to be taken out and examined in detail.

Physically, Lily-Marie was the epitome of everything feminine that turned me on. The long, blond hair. The pretty dresses. The curves I wanted to trace with my hands. The throaty voice that made me wonder what she sounded like first thing in the morning before her head even left the pillow.

So there I was, attracted to her and wanting to be her hero, bandaging her finger like I was performing open-heart surgery. And then she threw scissors at me and I didn't know if I'd been bewitched by Freddy Krueger.

If that wasn't whiplash enough, then she flashed me her panties and I found out her perfect curves extended to her thighs. She preferred comfortable underwear, like I would expect a stereotypical mom to choose, but they were also in a pretty pink. Like she had a flair for femininity that just couldn't be denied.

Did I really know Lily-Marie? Why was she acting so weird yesterday? And should I let my son ride to school with her?

I rolled out of bed and pulled on a pair of gray sweatpants. As I shaved in my bathroom, I came to the conclusion that I could be attracted to her all I wanted, but I needed to reassess things this morning before I let Stein get in her car. We'd agreed to start carpooling today, but I had to protect the most precious thing in the world to me: my son. If she was acting weird again this morning, I'd come up with an excuse to take him myself.

Pink panties or not, I had a responsibility.

"Come on, Dad, we're gonna be late!" Stein raced through the house with his backpack bouncing around behind him as he ran.

"All right, all right," I mumbled as I followed behind, smoothing down my hair and reminding myself to ignore how beautiful Lily-Marie might look this morning and be objective.

By the time I shut the front door behind me, Stein was over by the neighbor's SUV talking about something exciting with Clark. Their arms were flying all over as they got into it, whatever it was. Or maybe they both just had to pee. Milly was jumping up and down, trying to get either boy's attention to no avail.

A slamming door had my head turning to see Lily-Marie exiting her front door with a travel mug on top of a book, a purse on one shoulder, and a full tote bag hooked on the other arm. She was trying to lock the front door, but was about as successful as Milly when she tried to play with the older boys.

I walked over and took the book and mug out of her hand. She glanced over and blew some hair out of her face, a quick smile her morning greeting.

"Thanks. Don't know why I'm always rushing on Monday." She flipped the lock and threw her keys in her purse. Turning fully toward me, she took a deep breath. "I'm sorry about yesterday. I'll try to explain later, but right now I have to get these kids to school."

Something about her facing her embarrassment and addressing her odd behavior yesterday put me instantly at ease. Ignoring it like the behavior was normal would have been a bad sign. So I went with my gut.

I backed away and nodded. "Totally understand. See you here at drop-off?"

"You bet. Have a killer Monday." She flashed that broad grin and rushed past me, urging the kids to get in and buckle up.

I stood straddling our property line and waved them off. I stayed until the car turned the corner and could no longer be seen.

"I wonder..." I muttered out loud, rubbing my chin and finding a spot I missed while shaving. A more important thought than my questionable grooming habits occurred to me as I stood there: was Lily-Marie acting weird because money was so tight she couldn't afford to buy clothes? Making them was her only option? She was always wearing these beautiful sundresses. Maybe she made them all. She was a single mother, after all.

Maybe I needed to reassure her that there was nothing shameful about being frugal or making your own clothes. In fact, I admired her ingenuity. Instead of backing out of her front door yesterday, afraid for my safety, I should have been setting her mind at ease.

I ran inside my house and grabbed my laminated sheet off the kitchen counter. The list of fifty ways specifically said to take the woman clothes shopping. Well, it said to do it for a date, but I didn't see how we could do that with three kids between us. We'd just have to take them with us.

Mind made up, I finished getting ready and climbed in my car to head to the college. My mind was spinning, but one thing was for sure: I had to set things right by being a gentleman.

I heard car doors slamming, which brought me out of my curriculum building for the new biochem level-three class I wanted to offer in the fall. Shutting my laptop, I hopped up and ran outside, stiff from sitting all day, both at school and in my home office.

Stein came walking across the lawn. "Hey, Dad." He threw me a toothy grin, but kept walking to our house, probably to eat his habitual after-school snack. Seeing that he was home safe and acting normal, my gaze left him to settle on Lily-Marie gathering her things from the back of the car. I scanned her from head to toe, not to be a Neanderthal thinking a pretty woman was there for my viewing enjoyment—though I did enjoy it—but to see if I could discern if my homemade clothes theory was accurate.

Both of her kids had already jumped out of the car too, running inside leaving just the two of us. She was wearing one of the dresses I'd come to expect from her: soft, feminine, gorgeous. She had shapely calves that led down to tiny feet in a cork wedge heel, making her taller than she really was. I didn't know why the combination worked, but it set my heart rate into a gallop.

"The eagles are in the nest," Lily-Marie said with her head still in the back of her car.

I frowned. "There are eagles around here?"

Her head pulled out of the car and she smiled at me. "No, silly. It's a phrase. You know? Like the kids are back home?"

Oh. "I got it now. An idiom." I shoved my hands in my pockets and rocked back on my heels. I needed to hurry up and ask her to go shopping before I ruined yet another conversation with my awkwardness.

"Ohh...we got ourselves an English professor now?" Lily-Marie gave me a saucy grin and a wink, both of which hit my solar plexus the same as a physical blow.

"I-I'm sorry. I was deep into a biochem book when you got home and my brain sometimes takes a few minutes to catch up to normal conversation." I felt a moment of relief from having explained myself, then realized I'd phrased my offhand comment as if we lived together, sharing a mutual "home." I sucked in a deep breath and hoped she didn't take it that way. "Here, let me help you."

Lily-Marie handed off her large tote bag, which seemed to be as heavy as the bag of science textbooks I was always bringing home. "Thanks. I have a bunch of paperwork to go through tonight. Our department is trying to go paperless, but getting to that point takes a lot of scanning and shredding, you know?"

I nodded, understanding completely, as that was something most colleges were doing as well. Following her up the driveway, I decided to just throw it out there. Couldn't be any more awkward than anything else I'd ever said in front of her. "So. I was wondering if you and the kids wanted to go shopping with Stein and me soon. He needs some new clothes and we always end up arguing over what to buy. I figure if we make it something fun with you guys it won't be such a chore. What do you say?"

She opened the front door for me and let me walk inside before dropping her purse and keys on the entry table. "Sure. Probably the weekend would be best." She pulled off her jacket and hung it on a hook. "I bet Clark and Milly could use a few things too."

I nodded, inordinately pleased she'd said yes. The bar stool chair looked like the best place to unload a ridiculous amount of paperwork. My back was still turned when I casually added, "Maybe we can find you some things too."

Immediate silence behind me told me she'd either left the room or I hadn't been very sly with my comment. In my extensive experience, the answer to most troubling questions was usually "user error." I'd always had a hard time connecting with people in a real way. My words tripped over themselves on the way out of my mouth to land in a clumsy heap in front of my intended recipient. I'd come to expect it, but I'd never had a visceral loathing of my inability to converse naturally like I did in that moment.

I spun around to see Lily-Marie staring at me, eyes guarded, head cocked to the side. "That's a strange comment," she said slowly.

I tried valiantly to assemble the words in my head before they left my mouth, but as they say, "go big or go home." Like rogue soldiers, the words jumped ship and rearranged, dumping a stinking pile of nonsense at her feet. "Well, you were making a skirt. And you're a mom. So, I figured some shopping would be helpful." I winced.

I'm no expert when it comes to women, but her hand fisting

on her hip and the arch of one eyebrow said things were about to get ugly.

"I'm sorry, what?" She inhaled quickly and I guessed correctly again that was a rhetorical question. She unleashed and I took the hits. "Because I'm a mom I need help picking out clothes? You don't like the way I dress? 'Cause I'm pretty sure I never asked your opinion on what I choose to wear on my own body. And just because I was making a skirt doesn't mean I'm hard up for clothes. I was making a skirt to catch a man. The last thing I need is to go shopping with an egotistical male who will influence my young daughter with stupid ideas like needing a man to pick out your clothes because her own opinion isn't valid."

She shook her head and seemed to be collecting more weapons in this verbal warfare I found myself in. I had to jump in before this went from bad to worse. I flung my hands out in the universal sign of peace.

"No. Stop. Please. That's not what I meant. I would never insinuate that you need my opinion. I happen to love everything you wear, if you someday ask for my opinion. You have to understand. I don't say things right. I never have." I ran a hand through my hair, upsetting my carefully pomaded hairstyle. I was begging for her to understand, not even pausing to wonder why her impression of me mattered so much. "I just wanted to help. You're a single mom and if you couldn't afford clothes, I didn't want to stand by and do nothing. I just wanted to help. That's all."

She took a deep breath and the fire left her eyes with her exhale. She dropped my gaze for a moment before swinging it back and granting me a single nod. "Apology accepted. I'm sorry I jumped to conclusions. But I'm not hurting for money nor do I need you to buy me clothes."

I took a step closer. "Understood. And you're not the only conclusion jumper. Next time I'll just ask before coming up with weird ideas." My heart was pounding like I'd ridden twenty miles on my bike. I was awkward, but persistent. "Any chance you're still on for shopping, though? I wasn't kidding about Stein needing clothes. And it would be nice to spend some time together." A bead of sweat dripped down the center of my lower back.

A tilt to her lips and then a full smile took over her face, letting the sunshine come out again. "Yes, shopping sounds great. How about Friday night? The kids don't go to their dad's until Saturday morning."

Now that the ceasefire was called, I should have been ecstatic to escape without a scrape. But my chest felt heavy, like something was off. It wasn't until I said my goodbyes and walked to her door to head back to my place that it came to me. *I was making a skirt to catch a man.*

What the hell?

I froze as her words reverberated through my brain. One hand on the doorknob and not one rational thought to be found pinging around in there. My brain scrambled like my words and my body followed suit, acting like that of a robot. Reaching up to my shirt cuff, I grabbed a button and pulled. A discreet cough and the button was off without a sound. I let it slip through my fingers and fall to the floor, pinging off the tile and over my shoe. It rolled until it hit the wall by the door, falling over and coming to a stop.

Lily-Marie, having been behind me as we walked to her door, followed the path of the button and then stooped to pick it up. She flipped it over in her hand and then eyed my shirt. I was like a deer in headlights. The woman had more intelligence in her pinky finger than I had in my whole brain, science degrees or not. There was no way she was going to fall for the fact that my button had magically come off my shirt. I wasn't that good of an actor.

"Are you missing a button?" She trailed a finger down my torso, my muscles jumping and convulsing beneath her simple touch. I would have answered her if I still had breath in my body. She didn't wait for a response, simply grabbing my hands and examining my cuffs, finally seeing the empty spot where threads

71

dangled in the air. "Aha! Here. Damn mass-manufactured shirts these days. Always dropping buttons and seams coming unraveled."

She released my wrist and held the button out toward me. Time to go for broke. I rubbed the back of my neck. Anything to stop the tingling in my arm from where she held me. "Yeah, thanks. Um, any chance you could help me sew it back on? Seeing as how you're good with a needle and thread."

Her gaze whipped up and behind the guardedness from earlier, I could see a hint of pleasure. The tiny lines around her eyes relaxed and smoothed over at the compliment. She finally nodded. "Sure, I can do that for you. Just—"

All I heard was "sure" and I started unbuttoning my shirt right then and there.

"What—what are you doing?" Her mouth dropped open.

I continued unbuttoning and then took the shirt off, revealing the tight white undershirt below. How else was she going to sew it back on? I was pretty sure she couldn't do it while I was still in the shirt. "Giving you my shirt so you can sew the button on."

Her eyes darted back and forth across my chest and if I wasn't hallucinating, I could see a soft blush spreading across her cheeks.

She accepted the balled- up shirt from my outstretched hand and chuckled. "Clothes keep coming off when we see each other..."

ily-Marie

"So I wore the skirt and not one man at work said anything to me. A lady from accounting complimented me in the break room, though."

"And how old was she?" Gabby asked me over the phone.

I grimaced. "Close to retirement," I mumbled.

A bark of laughter had me pulling the phone from my ear. I got defensive. "Listen. So far, most of these fifty ways to find a husband have been total duds, but the Band-Aid thing totally worked. Just happened around the wrong man. I gotta keep going, Gabby. Besides, getting a new skirt out of the deal is better than being pickpocketed, so I'd have to rate my methods better than those stupid dating apps so far. Don't you think?"

Gabby had calmed down enough to listen. "I will give you that. But I still don't hold out much hope of you finding success with this scheme of yours. I'm sorry. I love you and I want you to be happy, but following advice from the 1950s seems a little cray-cray."

I pulled the phone from my mouth and shouted up the stairs, "Clark! You better be reading right now." When I heard a grunt in response, I went back to talking to Gabby. "I know it's a little crazy, but I'm willing to do whatever I need to, to find Mr. Right. Can't ding me for trying."

"Girl, you gotta let me write this stuff up in my column. Pretty please? I promise you it'll be anonymous and complimentary toward you. I've already written up three articles and I just need to hit submit to send them to my editor to get the series going."

I rubbed my forehead. She'd been lobbying hard to use my dating dilemmas for her newspaper for a while now and I just couldn't say no anymore. My defenses were low. "Fine. Submit it." I raised my voice over her loud whooping. "But make sure you keep details out that could ever be traced back to me. Promise?"

"I vow on my firstborn child—whenever that might be—to protect you. Thank you, Lil. This docu-series is going to go viral, I can feel it."

I rolled my eyes. *Viral*. "Yeah, whatever, just make sure you remember me in your acceptance speech of whatever awards they give to newspaper columnists."

"Uh, there are no awards."

"Well, shit. I guess I'll take a rain check. I kinda like you owing me one." It was my turn to giggle, but she was all business and didn't even acknowledge the imbalance of favors owed.

"Okay, so tell me about your latest interactions with Jameson."

I shook my head. "I'm not trying to marry Jameson, nor am I using my list where he's concerned. Forget him. Let's talk about my next moves."

"Nah-uh. Back up and tell me about Jameson and then tell me your next moves."

I sighed and rolled my eyes again, but went over all the

awkwardness with Jameson, leaving out the muscles I'd felt and seen when I'd touched him and he took his shirt off the other day. That part was irrelevant and quite frankly, embarrassing. When I'd tried to watch *Beauty and the Beast* last night before bed, I'd actually been comparing Gaston's physique to Jameson's. When I realized what I was doing, I turned it off and proceeded to toss and turn for far too long. His buttonless shirt sat on my dining table, mocking me.

"Hmm."

That was all Gabby said when I got done with my Jameson interactions. Which was strange. She usually had a litany of commentary, even when I didn't want it. When the silence stretched out, I launched into the stuff that mattered: my next moves.

"So, I looked up the fire stations around here and I Googled how to safely have my car break down on purpose. Jameson is picking the kids up from school tomorrow, so I'll use that free time to see if I can snag the attention of a hot firefighter." I got a little thrill just thinking about that one.

This was another reason I'd made up my mind to try this little husband-finding experiment. I wanted to have some adventure. I wanted some old-fashioned, innocent ways to meet a man. Well, mostly innocent. Aside from my fake car problems. What would a little white lie matter at our fiftieth wedding anniversary, you know?

At my advanced age of thirty-two I didn't even care so much about looks. I mean, I did, let's be real. But what I really wanted was a good, solid man to make me his everything. And what better place to find a selfless man than at a fire station?

"Oh, Lils. I sure hope this doesn't backfire." Gabby barked out another laugh. "Get it? Backfire?"

I snorted. "You're a legit comedian, Gabs."

Silence.

"Hello?" I asked when she didn't answer. "You still there?"

"Sorry. Just writing up article number four already. Gotta go, babe."

"Yeah, okay, love you too. Thanks for wishing me luck." My sarcasm must not have registered because all I heard was a soft click as she hung up. Dang, she was super focused on the article series. I hoped I hadn't miscalculated when I said yes. I had kids to think of. I'd have to move in the middle of the night and put them in new schools if people found out I was the subject of her stupid *viral* docu-series.

I sat at the curb, my SUV idling for ten minutes before the gas light came on. Thankfully, the fancy gadgets in cars these days tell you exactly how many miles you can go with the gas that was left in the tank. Looking at my maps app, the fire station was 9.6 miles away. When the car dash said ten miles was left in the tank, I pulled away from the curb and drove in the direction of the station.

Some would say this was stupid at best, dangerous at worst. But I had a cell phone with a full battery charge and I had pepper spray in my purse. And it was broad daylight in Costa Mesa. I was pretty sure I was as safe as any other day driving in SoCal traffic. Maybe some extra water would have been good in case of a long wait, but I had a bit of this morning's coffee in my travel mug. Now I just hoped the firefighters were all there at the station, not out at an actual emergency.

I sat forward and gripped the steering wheel until my knuckles turned white and my hands got slippery with sweat. Just as the station came into view, my car started to lurch. My eyes widened and I tried to control my breathing. I was a little shocked that this scheme of mine was going to work. At least the breaking down part.

Letting my foot off the gas, I coasted in front of the station right as my car gave one final jerk and stalled out. I put it in park and took one final deep breath. Time for my acting skills to take over. I looked around wildly and threw my hands up in the air like I just didn't care. No, wait. That was from some ridiculous song Clark listened to. I threw my hands up in the air like I didn't know what to do.

I was just about to hop out and pop the hood when there was a knock on my driver's side window. Nearly hit my head on the roof from jumping so badly. I placed a hand on my chest and cracked the window when I registered it was already one of the firefighters at my door.

"Having some car troubles, miss?" He flashed a smile and I wasn't having to act anymore. I was genuinely flustered and atwitter. Holy testosterone.

"Ah yes, yes, I am. Not sure what happened, but it just died on me."

Another brilliant smile. Damn, the man had a dimple. "Why don't you step out and I'll see what I can do."

I smiled what I hoped wasn't a devious grin. Forcing my movements to slow down so I didn't appear overeager, I grabbed my purse. He stepped back and I opened my door. Expecting cologne or a delicious sweaty male smell, I got a lungful of swamp. I nearly gagged. Looking down, I'd parked right over a storm drain. Just my luck.

Breathing through my mouth, I went to push up to standing when a work-roughened hand appeared in front of me. My smile grew as I placed my hand in his and accepted his help. I straightened up and looked up through my lashes to see Jameson standing before me, a frown pulling his dark eyebrows together.

I shook my head, thinking maybe I was dreaming. Or more like having a nightmare. Where was my dimpled hero?

"Jameson?" I pulled my hand from his and rubbed it against my prettiest dress, refusing to enjoy the way his skin felt against mine. I was thoroughly confused, but all I could think about was how nerdy Professor MacMillan managed to get callouses.

"I was just a few cars behind you with the kids when we saw your car pull off. What happened?"

Hyperaware of an audience, I swiveled my head and found the firefighter back up on the curb, his arms crossed over his chest, watching our interaction, dimple nowhere to be found. One of his buddies walked out of the station to stand by his side. It was like a factory of hot men in there, spitting out a new one every few minutes. Dammit, Jameson!

"Um, well, I'm not sure. It just kind of died."

His hands landed on my hips and he just kind of placed me out of the way so he could climb into my car. I wasn't sure how I felt about being moved like that.

"When was the last time you gassed this thing up?" he called loudly from inside the capsule.

Heat flared on my face, especially when the two firefighters started smirking.

"Mom? Did you forget to put gas in the car again?" my oldest evil spawn yelled from Jameson's car where the windows were rolled down. All three kids had their heads sticking out the windows watching the drama unfold.

"Uh, not sure?" I couldn't help the way my voice tilted up at the end there, making it obvious I was a twit, not a full-grown woman capable of taking care of the basics with her own damn car. I heard a stifled laugh from the direction of the firefighters. Why was there always an audience to my humiliation?

"Tell your husband we have some gas cans in the station. We'll get you back on the road, don't worry." Mr. Dimples smiled, spun on his heels, and hustled back into the station.

"He's not my..." I trailed off, realizing it wasn't even worth protesting. A girl needed to know when she was defeated and I was so there I'd set up house with a house plant and a cat named Merle.

Jameson climbed out of the car and cocked his head, just staring at me.

"What?" I snapped.

His eyes narrowed, but he said, "Nothing."

The firefighter came back, gas can in hand. He tipped it into my gas tank and filled it up enough to get me to the nearest gas station. He shook Jameson's hand, in some old-school "took care of the little lady for you" gesture. He simply acknowledged me with a nod and walked away. I guess I shouldn't have expected a more modern reaction when I myself was trying an old-fashioned way to meet a man. I couldn't have it both ways.

"I'll follow you to the gas station to make sure you get there all right." Jameson held my car door open and waited for me to get in before shutting it and walking back to his vehicle, which held my children.

So that was that.

Defeat smelled an awful lot like a backed-up storm drain and day-old coffee.

No firefighter's phone number. No date. No flirting.

It was looking more and more like I'd need all fifty ways to land myself a husband. Five down, forty-five to go.

The Reality of Love, Mom-Com Style - episode #4

Thank you, dear reader, for your enthusiastic opinions on our girl, Betty's, dating life. I've read each and every one of your tweets. As promised, here's your daily update.

An interesting contender is bubbling up while Betty is searching for Mr. Right. Perhaps he's Mr. Right Next Door.

It's the age-old romance situation. Everything you need can be found in the boy/girl next door if you'd only see what was right in front of you. But you know what they say: when the student is ready, the teacher will appear. Until then, let's follow Betty searching fruitlessly all over town for the one to sweep her off her feet.

And we'll be sure to keep an eye on the leading man.

Hot Neighbor: 1

Betty: 0

10

ameson

I've given plenty of icy glares to recalcitrant students in my teaching career, but I've never been on the receiving end of one quite so glacial as the one Lily-Marie gave me when we finally caravanned home after finding her stranded on the road. Which struck me as extremely odd, considering I'd helped her out of a tough situation. No man or woman wanted to be stranded with car troubles. That's why we all had car insurance and AAA cards in our wallets taking up valuable space where another maxed-out credit card could have gone.

In my line of work, when something didn't make sense, you sat down and traced back what happened. You pulled it apart to its basic parts and examined each one. So as I sat there Friday afternoon in my home office, waiting for Stein to get home from school, I dissected each and every word of our exchange in front of the fire station. Every glance, every look, every possible outlier.

And my only conclusion was that Lily-Marie simply didn't like me.

It shouldn't have come as a surprise. I wasn't really the kind of guy who inspired enthusiastic friendships or grand love affairs. I was steady. I was purposeful. When I did things, they made sense. When someone helped me, I thanked them.

But Lily-Marie not liking me? That started an ache in my chest that a couple Tums I popped in my mouth didn't seem to touch. Did she only agree to go shopping together because she pitied me? Hell, that felt even worse than simply not liking me. I pushed back from my desk and walked away from the papers that weren't getting graded anyway while I sat there and ruminated on Lily-Marie's reaction.

I walked into the kitchen and grabbed a bottle of water out of the fridge. I gulped it down and pondered what to do with this new conclusion. Should I cancel shopping tonight? Should I go through with it and ask her what the deal was? Maybe my conclusion was wrong and I just needed to push harder with my fifty ways.

The thing was, a scientist never quits the experiment unless something horrific was happening and for safety reasons it needed to be shut down. Other than my feelings being squashed, nothing horrible had happened. I needed to complete the experiment to the best of my ability. And really, every reaction of Lily-Marie's simply proved my original hypothesis correct. A man could do all the right things to show a woman he cared and it still wouldn't be enough to make them fall in love. That kind of love just didn't exist.

I placed the empty water bottle in the recycling bin and walked back into my office to grab my laminated sheet. Firing my computer back up, I opened up my notes about the experiment. Pecking away furiously with two index fingers, I typed out our exchange last night and then glanced at the sheet to see which ways I could try that night during the shopping excursion.

Complimenting her seemed like a good one as she might be trying on new clothes. I could show her I was well-read with interesting topics of conversation. Holding her coat and opening doors for her was a given. We were going shopping, so that was another one right there. I mean really, if I was going to go full steam ahead with the experiment, I should pack as many ways into each interaction as possible, right?

Maybe that's where I'd gone wrong previously. I only tried out one at a time. Maybe the trick to this whole thing was doing a bunch all at once.

With renewed hope filling my chest, I read through the list multiple times, trying to memorize it and plan out how to accomplish them all in one night. Thank God Grandmother didn't do a list of a *hundred* ways to find a wife!

Lily-Marie had been perfectly at ease with me the minute we climbed into my car to carpool to Fashion Island. While the kids squabbled in the back, I'd asked some perfectly normal questions on the ride over about some fiction books I'd read recently, showing her I wasn't a stilted science professor, which turned out to be a good topic for her. She admitted to being quite the reader and I was intrigued to see that she read all kinds of genres. The *Lee Child* series being a personal favorite was something we had in common. She also admitted to a love of young adult books that I had yet to give a try. We hadn't written it in stone, but she insinuated she'd come over with *The Hunger Games* DVDs and we'd watch those together. She was intent on winning me over to the dark side of YA. If it made her smile again like she did as she talked about it, I was all in.

A loud shriek pierced the close confines of the car right before I turned into the parking lot. The kids had gotten louder and louder on the way over, my own child being the ring leader of noise.

I preferred a much quieter environment, but I didn't want to reprimand Stein in front of Lily-Marie as that was one of the fifty ways I was to be minding. The list said not to scold the kids too harshly in front of a woman. So I winced with every shriek and bit my tongue.

Lily-Marie started throwing glances to the back and fidgeting with her purse strap. I finally pulled into a parking space and cut the engine.

"Stein." I didn't yell. My tone said "no nonsense," but I was sure to keep my volume moderate.

"What, Dad?" He instantly stopped badgering Clark and faced forward.

"You know what." I tossed him "the look" over my shoulder and then climbed out of the car. The minute my feet hit the pavement, I broke into a run and rounded the back of the car to come around the passenger side and pull open Lily-Marie's door. She looked up, startled, but then thanked me as she got out. Warmth flooded my chest at her approval. Maybe she did like me.

We ushered the kids into a higher-end department store and found the kids' section first. After piling them up with clothes to try on, Lily-Marie and I sat on a bench in the empty dressing room hall and had the boys try on their clothes first. Milly had a few of her tiny dolls with her and played in front of the huge three-way mirror at one end of the dressing room. Stein was the first to come out in one of the pairs of pants he'd chosen.

"Oh, honey, I don't know. I think the striped capris might be a little too out there. I prefer the dark gray jeans you picked out." Lily-Marie, God bless her, was the voice of reason and Stein actually listened to her, just shrugging and going back into his dressing room to change.

I looked over at her incredulously, conscious of how close we were sitting. I could smell the faint citrus layer of her perfume and feel her body move when she shifted on the bench. All I wanted was to scoot just a bit closer. In science-speak, we were water: our hydrogen bonds caused our molecules to be highly attracted to each other.

"Why are you looking at me like that?"

I blinked and tried to pull my thoughts together. "What?"

She chuckled, her blue eyes sparkling and alive. "You're looking at me like I'm the Mother Teresa of clothes shopping."

I shrugged, latching on to the excuse she'd given me. I couldn't very well tell her I wanted to covalent bond with her. "Well, you did just get Stein to put back those ridiculous pant things without a yelling match ensuing. So I'd say you're more Gandhi, bringing peace to the MacMillan household."

She threw back her head and laughed. I silently vowed to spend the whole night complimenting her just to witness that unleashed joy again.

"So, what are you trying on tonight, Ms. Masters?" Lingerie? Nightgowns? Short shorts? A guy could dream, couldn't he?

She shrugged off my question. "I don't really need anything. I just have work clothes and casual clothes for around the house. Got plenty of both."

I rubbed my chin, thinking. "Milly?"

Her little blond head popped up from her dolls, a ready smile on her face, so similar to her mother's.

"How about you and your mommy try on some fancy dresses?"

Her face lit up and she abandoned her precious dolls to race over, climbing onto my lap and stealing my heart in the process. "Can we weally?"

I grinned at her enthusiasm, ignoring Lily-Marie's groan in my ear. "It'll be super fun, won't it, Mommy?"

Milly clapped her hands, bouncing on my lap. "We'll be like the princesses in the movies we watch together!"

I knew there was no way Lily-Marie could say no to both

of us.

She rolled her eyes, but a smile played across her mouth. "All right, all right. I do like a good Disney princess movie. Count me in."

Lily-Marie helped Milly climb off my lap and they left to find ball gowns to try on. The boys came out with more outfit choices, most of which we decided were a "no." Turns out having Clark there was just as helpful as Lily-Marie. He kept Stein away from his more ridiculous choices. My poor kid just had no fashion sense whatsoever. His sense of self-preservation in the social scene of pre-pubescent boys was clearly missing.

As the boys grabbed the few items we wanted to purchase, I decided to pump intel from Clark to help me get to know Lily-Marie better. "So, Clark, what's this I hear about the women in your family loving princess movies?"

He rolled his eyes. Like mother, like son. "It's mostly Mom. I mean, Milly likes them too, but Mom is a nut for all things Disney princesses. She watches them all the time. Knows all the songs by heart. I swear, she's single because she's looking for Prince Charming. I keep telling her it's just a movie. It doesn't happen for real."

He and Stein put their items on the counter and while the clerk rang them up, I let his words roll around in my head. So, she wanted a Prince Charming, huh? What did he have that I didn't? Besides the fact he was a fictional cartoon character. Sadly, I hadn't watched too many of those princess movies growing up or as an adult. I'd have to do some research to figure out the charac-teristics of Lily-Marie's perfect man.

"Guys?"

The woman who wouldn't stop running through my mind was right behind us, dresses hanging over her arm and nearly grazing the floor. Milly was grinning from ear to ear and tugging on her mother's purse. Lily-Marie looked a little frazzled with her flushed cheeks barely showing above the huge stack of clothing.

"Wow, you trying on the whole store, Mom?" Clark asked, laughing.

"These aren't all for me!" she defended herself.

I grinned, the very idea of seeing her in any of those dresses all that could penetrate my thoughts. "Why don't you and Milly get started and I'll meet you in there?"

"But I need to pay for Clark's things." She looked like she was attempting to shift the dresses, which everyone but her could see would be a disaster.

"No, no! We'll settle up at dinner."

"Dinner?" She froze.

"Yeah. Dinner. All this shopping has made us hungry." I hadn't actually asked the boys if they were hungry.

"We're starved!" Stein nearly shouted.

Pre-teen boys. Of course they were hungry.

"Go. I got the boys." I waved her off and she finally relented, probably because Milly looked like she either had to pee or she was about to burst from her excitement about the dresses.

I finished paying for the boys' clothes and then found them some chairs in the shoe department to sit in while they waited for the ladies. They were under strict orders not to move from those chairs and to keep the noise down. Their innocent upturned faces didn't fool me. If I didn't have a page over the intercom asking for their parents to come get them before the night was out, I'd be surprised.

I hustled to make it back to the dressing room. I wanted to see every single dress Lily-Marie tried on. Thankfully, we were still the only shoppers in this particular fitting room. I could see Lily-Marie's wedges from beneath the stall door.

"Got one on?" I called.

A tiny giggle and then an awed "wow" came from behind the closed door. My heart was beating superfast and it suddenly felt imperative to see Lily-Marie in a fancy ball gown.

"Let me see," I called again impatiently.

The door cracked open with a groan. My breath caught in my chest and out stepped the most gorgeous five-year-old princess I'd ever seen. Milly looked up at me with a shy smile, twisting back and forth where she stood in a soft pink satin dress. A big bow was tied behind her and the skirt portion of the dress had some sort of glittery stuff on it that danced in the overhead lights. Feeling like what I said in that moment could make or break a young girl's heart, I chose my words carefully, making sure they would come out right this time.

"You forgot one thing, beautiful girl."

She tilted her head.

"Where's your crown, Princess?"

A grin took over her face and she launched herself at me, wrapping her little arms around my legs in the smallest of bear hugs. I patted her back and silently promised her all sorts of things that weren't my place to promise. Like a man to protect her and watch over her always. Someone to beat away the boys and show her exactly what she was worth.

The door groaned again, interrupting my train of thought and the rush of emotion pulling me under from a little girl's hug. Had I not been blindsided by the small bundle still attached to my legs, I would have remembered the whole point of coming in here and suggesting ball gowns was to see Lily-Marie in one.

As it was, I startled when she pulled the door fully open and smiled down at Milly, her eyes misting over. I understood the tears: her daughter was absolutely adorable. What I couldn't seem to comprehend was the blast of desire I felt seeing Lily-Marie in a turquoise floor-length dress. If the wall hadn't been behind me, I would have fallen backward from the blow.

The material clung to her like a second skin, showing off her tiny waist, before flaring out and falling to the ground in a wave of silk. Thin straps held the top up, but not before pressing her breasts up and together, nearly spilling them over the neckline like a wave cresting.

If Milly looked like a princess, then her mother, in that dress, was certainly a queen.

"It's a little tight." Lily-Marie shimmied, adjusting the top, and I swallowed hard.

I seemed to be having an out-of-body experience there in the fitting room. I knew I should stop staring at her breasts. In fact, I was shouting at myself to avert my eyes, but my body wasn't responding. Well, it was responding, but not in the area where my eyes were located.

"It's horrible, isn't it?" Lily-Marie's voice held a hint of a waver, which was just the motivation I needed to bring myself back to my body. She couldn't be left to think she wasn't absolutely everything in that swath of silk.

My gaze flew to her face and I found her blushing hard, her hair piled on top of her head, leaving her neck deliciously free of her long locks. She looked highly uncomfortable standing there in her bare feet, which just didn't make sense. She was a damn vision in that dress. A stunner. A model. She should never wear anything else.

"N-no." I swallowed again and tried harder. "You look absolutely gorgeous. Perfect. Maybe the right word is ethereal. Queenly. Beyond this world."

Her eyes widened and her lips lost their downturn. I patted my back, gave myself a gold star, awarded myself a raise. I'd said something to make her stop doubting herself. My epic triumph caused my chest to pound all the way up to the top of my head.

Then she smiled full out and that's when I knew.

I was wrong.

This experiment wasn't failing, per se. It was just designed poorly. In a bizarre twist of fate—and science—the intended highway of feelings flowed the wrong direction. The list of fifty ways to find a wife wasn't making Lily-Marie fall for me.

I was falling for *Lily-Marie.*

ily-Marie

I shifted from foot to foot, absorbing what Jameson had said. He thought I was ethereal? That was high praise from a stilted science professor. Maybe he moonlighted as an English professor occasionally.

I wasn't oblivious. I saw him staring at my breasts, and I mean, really, how could he not? They were practically on display at an exhibition in this tight dress and glaring overhead lights. But then he looked at me and I could have sworn I saw *awe* in his gaze. I couldn't tell you the last time a man had looked at me with reverence.

Maybe never.

And though I'd sworn Jameson wasn't for me, I melted a bit right there in the dressing room. His compliments held weight, turning them from an "aw-shucks" moment to his opinion weaving into the fabric of what I believed about myself. I felt myself standing taller, sucking it in less, admiring the curves I saw in the mirror behind him rather than looking at them with disdain.

Before I could even formulate an answer, the boys rushed in, a bubble of excitement, their words overlapping each other.

"Whoa, there. What's going on?" Jameson jumped in and I appreciated him calming them down. In the car, the kids had gotten a little out of control and I kept waiting for him to say something to them, but he'd kept quiet until the very end.

Clark put his hand on Stein's arm, taking the lead. "We were sitting in the shoe department, where you told us to stay, but then we saw a guy walk by with the new Gucci shirt Beckham wore last week on Instagram. So, we asked him where he got it and we went and got you one to try on."

"Yeah, Dad! Try it on. We all got to try on clothes, but you didn't. This shirt is, like, *everything*." Stein handed it to Jameson like it was the crown jewels when it was really only a hideous red plaid shirt with green camouflage on the collar and cuffs. Like two different shirts got in a tussle and decided to just blend together to settle their differences.

Jameson took the hanger from the boy and eyed it like you would a skunk: with caution. "Wow, a shirt that's *everything*, huh? I should definitely try it on."

Jameson stepped right in front of me and hooked the hanger on the door behind my head. I tried to scooch out of his way, but with the door behind me, there was nowhere to go. Starting at the top, Jameson unbuttoned the shirt he had on, the most confident smirk I'd ever seen gracing his face. Only a few buttons in and I knew what was going on.

He had no undershirt on below.

So, with each button, a new inch or two of tan skin was revealed. And oh, what a torso of skin it was.

Someone somewhere cranked the heater and I was afraid I'd

have to buy the damn ball gown because I started to sweat in it. You leave bodily fluids, you buy it.

Then he was ripping the shirt off and muscles I didn't know the man had were rippling and moving and stretching like I had my own not-so-private striptease. Shoulder boulders that dipped into biceps that had seen a curl or two. My gaze drifted over his chest, two mountains I suddenly had the urge to squeeze with my bare hands. And then, the body part I'd never actually seen up close before.

Even with all the visual porn, I was aware my kiddos were in the room and I bet he knew it too, so no, he didn't flash me *that* body part. More the shame. What I meant was, I saw an actual six-pack of ab muscles. Previously, I'd only been witness to your typical dad-bod midsection. Even with all the boys I'd seen at the pool or at the beach in high school, well before those boys had become dads, I'd only seen sub-par abs that didn't hint at any sort of sections. It was just one large, soft area of belly.

This... Well, this was an actual six-pack with valleys in between the bulges of muscle, and let me tell you, for research purposes only, I counted them. One, two, three, four, five, six. The man had a six-pack.

No sooner had I verified the count than he put the hideous shirt on and covered it all up again. My eyes went from over-heating from visual perfection to nearly crossing at the clash of colors and patterns.

"You totally have to buy it, Dad!" Stein shouting his approval brought me out of my ab-induced haze. I blinked several times and saw Milly staring up at Jameson with stars in her eyes. Apparently, she didn't mind the ugliest shirt known to the twenty-first century. She was taken by Jameson for entirely different reasons than her mother.

When I'd come out of the dressing room after hearing him call her a princess and saw her hugging him so fiercely, my heart had squeezed in my chest. As a mother, you want to give your children the best of everything and it's the very worst of guilt trips to realize you saddled them forever with a not-so-good father. Yes, he still saw them nearly every weekend, but he just wasn't engaged with them. Milly never looked at Shawn with stars in her eyes. I would bet Shawn had never taken her shopping or insisted she try on ball gowns.

I'd have to watch Milly carefully to make sure she didn't grow too attached to Jameson. He was just the next-door neighbor. He had no ties to her and could move again at any moment.

"While I'm tempted, Lily-Marie looks like she smells something foul, so I'm going to have to pass." Jameson's voice interrupted my thoughts.

Everyone swiveled their head to look at me. That's when I realized I'd been frowning, lost in my thoughts.

"Sorry! It's interesting. Just not quite your colors." I tilted my head like I was actually considering the shirt, trying to let Stein down easy.

Jameson clapped. "Okay, that's resolved. I'm starving! Let's go eat, huh?"

The kids all jumped into action, Milly tugging my arm to go back into the dressing room and get out of her beautiful dress. I let her pull me back in, but not before a backward glance to catch one last sight of Jameson as he took his shirt off. I only counted to four before the door slammed shut and Milly demanded to be unzipped. Such was the life as a mom.

By the time I got Milly and myself out of our dresses and we'd herded the kids to a restaurant next door, I'd cooled off, placing the vision of bare-chested Jameson in a box in the back of my brain never to be brought out again. Because the reality was, he wasn't the man for me. I wasn't settling again for a nice guy who was just okay who'd eventually leave me for a younger, thinner, prettier model. I wanted the magic. I wanted to be swept off my feet and treasured. Jameson was a nice guy, and okay, I admit, he had some delicious abs, but he wasn't my Prince Charming in his polos and sweaters and stilted conversational skills.

I know, that was a bit harsh. He'd told me himself he had a hard time saying the right thing, but the dating world was harsh too. I needed to refocus and put my moves on some fresh potential mates, not drool over my neighbor. My libido needed redirecting and getting back on the horse quickly was the best way to get on with it. Great, now even my thoughts were as jumbled as that hideous shirt.

Jameson held the door open and the kids and I stepped into the waiting area of a barbecue joint, the smells hitting us the minute we entered. My stomach growled and I was glad we abandoned shopping for sustenance. Jameson went up to the desk to put our name in while I scanned the people waiting for their tables.

A middle-aged man with a hint of gray at his temples sat on a bench lining the walls, next to a couple other guys. Clearly, the men were out for a night of barbecue and watching the football game. No ring on the left hand.

Game on, boys.

I sauntered over and claimed the seat right next to his, sliding close in the guise of needing room for the three kids who trailed me. I supposed trying to get my flirt on with my kids in tow ran a bit out of the ordinary, but better to get that little fact out of the way. If he had an issue with my kids, better to know now rather than later.

He shifted as I sat down, his head rotating to get a look at me. I smiled my warmest smile and followed him by closing the inch of gap he'd given us. His polite smile turned warmer. Before I could give him my opening line, the one I'd been working up in my head to be a doozy, rough hands hauled me up to standing.

I was chest to chest with Jameson, his familiar scowl

somehow shaming me for my seat choice. My hands were pinned between us, caught in his tight grip. Then the room was spinning and Jameson was in my seat, pulling me down to his lap, his hands on my hips giving me no choice.

Anger bubbled up my wind pipe, but got strangled by the sensation of being on Jameson's lap. My damn libido was barking up the wrong tree again and my intended victim—potential date—was walking off to be seated at his table, never to have heard my line that would have procured his number, I was sure of it.

I sat there, stunned, Jameson's tree trunk legs the perfect seat bottom, his chest the ideal back rest. My thoughts were conflicted. The commanding way he stepped in and moved me was kind of hot. The goal-oriented modern woman in me was pissed. How dare he get in the way of my flirting game? The anger won out, that and the fact that my kids were watching me sit on a man's lap—who wasn't Santa.

Scrambling off his lap, I sat down in the seat the silver fox had vacated, crossing my arms over my chest. I refused to look at Jameson. I didn't owe him an apology. As far as I was concerned, he owed me one.

"MacMillan, party of five?" The hostess called us and none too soon. As she led us to our table, I saw another man having dinner with a table full of guy friends. A streak of boldness rushed up my spine, making me roll my shoulders back and thrust my ample breasts out. Two could play this game.

Right as we passed, I pretended to stumble, catching myself on the man's strong shoulders. Not as wide as Jameson's, but why the hell was I comparing, anyway? He looked up and held me steady with one hand on my elbow.

"Sorry about that! Me and my two left feet." I gave him a winning smile, which he returned for a brief second. Until Jameson wrapped his arm around my shoulders and hustled me off to our table.

"Careful, honey," he said just a bit more loudly than necessary.

I jabbed an elbow in his gut with all my pent-up frustration behind it and sped off. I took a seat at our table right between my two children, which meant I wouldn't have to sit next to Jameson.

Dinner went fine as I kept up a lively conversation with the kids. Jameson interjected here and there, but otherwise left me alone. I stewed about his behavior the entire time we ate. He had no right to stop my flirting attempts. So why did he stop them? What was his deal? I thought he was still hung up on his ex. Did he somehow have feelings for me and I just didn't know it?

I'd like to state that I'm a mature woman, having mothered two kids already, but the thing was, I liked to have a little fun. Sometimes at other people's expense. Like when I purposely stood up from the table the other night just to see if Jameson would stand too. It gave me a little thrill. Kept some humor in my otherwise mundane and stressful life. It wasn't hurting anyone, so why not?

Which was why I decided to try as hard as I could to use another one of the ways to find a husband when we left the restaurant. Just to see what he'd do. A little test, if you will. After Jameson held the large wooden restaurant door open for me again, I walked through the parking lot with the kids behind me. Right as we passed a group of people standing around chatting, I zeroed in on the single guy—currently the only one in the group without a woman hanging on him—and made my move.

Without missing a beat, I tripped, yet again. Damn those two left feet of mine. I almost went down, but before I did, I caught myself. My purse, however, was not so fortunate. The force of my almost-fall slingshot that sucker into the air, flipping it upside down and upending everything that was in it. And I'm a mom, so you know it was a lot of crap that came raining down on the pavement, right at the feet of my intended target.

I heard the kids gasp behind me, but interestingly enough,

not a peep out of Mr. Muscles and Frowns. Thankfully, the guy I'd targeted did exactly what Ms. Sanders must have envisioned when she wrote up her man-list. He swooped down and instantly started picking up my various items like the gentleman he clearly was. I had a full three seconds of jubilation before Jameson squatted down and helped pick up the ten thousand things that were rolling around the ground.

"Gotta be more careful, darling," he chastised while picking up a tampon and putting it back in my purse.

The other guy immediately quit helping and just handed the things he'd collected to Jameson, like he had some claim over me and my things simply because he called me "darling." The guy nodded at me and went back to his group, all of whom were eyeing me like I was the crazy mom who'd had too much to drink at dinner and now was embarrassing her children in public. Little did they know it did not take alcohol nor the public sphere for me to embarrass them. This little show was all extra entertainment from a completely sober state. Which was sobering.

Next thing I knew, Jameson was leading me by the elbow to his car, reclaimed purse in hand.

"Was that really necessary?" he muttered quietly enough the kids couldn't hear.

I smiled devilishly to the side of his head, inordinately pleased with the frown that covered his face. "Oh, it really was."

"Hello?" Gabby's tired voice finally picked up after the third ring. Good thing too, as I was in my bed all snuggled up and ready to keep calling her ass all night until she answered.

"Get this. I'm getting cock-blocked by my next-door neighbor."

There was a pause. Then she was back, fully alert.

"Tell me everything."

~

Traipsing through the woods with a bounce in my step and in my turquoise floor-length ball gown, I see the leaves and bark on the trees as if in technicolor. Everything is so other-worldly beautiful I want to cry in appreciation. Little birds hop along the branches, trailing the larger squirrels as they follow in the wake of my path. I can't help but break into song, the clear, strong voice surprising me when I sound just like Aurora in Sleeping Beauty.

I sing from memory, words of searching for my prince, wondering where he is and when he'll find me. The sun filters down between the trees to spotlight me as I dance around, my feet floating over the pine needles and rocks.

A thundering out in the distance stops me cold. My hand flutters to my heart and all the forest animals run for cover. I stand there, unable to move, awaiting whatever is about to come through the brush and find me.

I don't feel scared, just curious, as if I'm right there in every tiny detail, but not really there at all.

Hooves beat out a cadence, like a song beat in my head. Crashing through the leaves arrives a huge white beast of a horse, his nostrils flaring as he breathes hard. My gaze travels up, up, up.

And I wonder no more.

My prince is here.

Sitting high on his steed is a stranger, yet he needs no introduction. Dark hair swoops back in an exaggerated coif, not a hair out of place despite the rough ride. Thick eyebrows scrunch together in a delicious frown that brings a shiver to my spine. He's handsome and virile, the perfect match for a girl like me.

He knows it too for he slows his beast and comes alongside me, the frown easing as he takes in my dress. Every glance is like a physical caress, making me weak in the knees, but strengthening my resolve to permit him anything and everything.

Finally he stops, his horse prancing in place, no longer something I fear. My prince would never let me come to harm.

"Your name, young lady?" His voice settles over me like a warm blanket. Familiar.

"Lily, Your Highness." I curtsy low to the ground and I pause a moment, wondering how I accomplished such a move. Straightening, I see his gaze flicker from my chest to my face and back. I should be embarrassed by the amount of cleavage showing in this ridiculous dress, but all I feel is elation at winning his attention.

"Come." His gloved hand stretches down to me, beckoning me to follow. I will not disobey his command. Not ever.

Placing my hand in his, he swings me up onto his quivering horse. I sit side saddle on his lap, bombarded by sensation being pressed against his wall of muscle, a hardness so different than mine.

His lips, only inches away, say my name. "Lily. You are mine."

There's no argument from me, which sets off a warning bell in the back of my head. I should protest, I know I should, yet all I do is nod, like it was never in question.

His hand releases mine to grab the reins. With a flick of the leather, we're off, back into the heart of the woods, where no one roams but me. And now my prince. When we arrive at a particularly dense section, he pulls the horse to a stop.

I look around quickly, seeing nothing familiar, but then again, it's almost entirely dark and I can't see anything save for the man I'm pressed up against. The horse's swaying begins to make me dizzy.

He drops the reins and slides his gloves off, one hand at a time. I'm mesmerized by his hands; the size of them, the shape, the rough-looking callouses that don't seem congruent with a prince. And then he's sweeping my long, blond hair to one side, a single fingertip tracing down my exposed neck to the cleavage begging to be freed.

My breath comes quick and shallow. His touch is fire, lighting up nerve endings that have lain dormant until now.

"Lily," he calls.

I open my eyes, not realizing I'd closed them. He's staring at me, those eyelids half closed, but not enough to hide the storm I see in the gray irises.

"Make your decision. Stay on the horse? Or against a tree?"

His words make no sense. But he's asked me to make a decision and I will. Anything my prince desires. So I pick, having no idea what about.

"Tree, please."

His arms bracket me against his chest and suddenly we're on the ground, the horse gone. It's only us and a forest of trees. He lifts me again and my hands fly to his shoulders. I have no doubt that he wouldn't drop me, but I can't wait any longer to touch him.

My back slams against a rough wall and a squeal squeezes out of my throat.

Against a tree.

"I need you, Lily," my prince groans into my neck.

Too lost for words, I nod my agreement and he kisses his way up to my jaw and then finally my mouth. His lips coax mine open, his tongue a plundering force like I've never experienced before. He's consuming me one kiss at a time.

A pull, a tug, down deep in my belly. I don't know what I want, but I want it all right now. With him.

"Wrap your legs around me, love," he whispers against my lips.

He helps me obey by pulling my long skirt to my waist. The chilled air hits my skin until he presses between my legs, no air possible between our bodies now. His kisses continue, this time accompanied by a flexing of his hips that sends shots of light behind my eyes. When he stops, I follow, my body too strung out on his drug to go without, even for a moment.

A loud rip enters my awareness, my panties a flash of bright yellow as they're flung to the ground. I nip at his bottom lip, my hands holding his face, desperate for more even as his hands leave my body.

A clink of metal rings out, echoing among the trees. I don't have long to wonder, not when his bare skin is now against my most inti-

mate space. It's heaven, it's hell. I need the sweet torment to end, but I already fear for when it does.

He enters me on an exhale, the sting momentary, the fullness my new obsession.

"Mine, Lily, mine," he chants. He pulls back and then plunges forward, my back taking the brunt of the force. The bark chafes and scrapes my delicate skin, but blinding pleasure exceeds any irritation.

"Please," I moan, for what I don't know, don't care.

He drives into me faster, the slide easier now, all pain gone entirely. A storm is brewing, too vast and dangerous to be survived. I know it, and yet I still race forward to meet it. I claw at his shoulders, squeezing my legs tighter, riding my prince with each long stroke and jarring bounce.

And then it breaks.

The storm clouds burst and rain down light, letting me see his face, a mask of concentration as he blunders my body. I throw my head back and ride out the aftermath, hearing his shout as he spills himself into me.

A smile is all that's left of me.

And when I wake, I still feel the pulsing between my thighs, the sting on my back, and the smile that may just be permanent now.

Until I realize who my prince was in my naughty dream.

Jameson.

My next-door neighbor.

12

ameson

My journal was open in front of me on my desk, waiting for me to document my science experiment progress, but I couldn't get myself to write anything down. Simply because my reaction to Lily-Marie and her reaction to me was nonsensical, which had no place in a scientific journal. I looked through the window in my office to the halls of the science lab surrounding me. I felt like I'd let the entire field of science down by not being able to place my relationship with Lily-Marie into a formula.

I slammed the journal closed and threw it into my satchel. Tuesday afternoons were supposed to be open office hours for me, but I couldn't stay stuck behind this desk any longer. I needed to move, to think, to process. Walking out of the building, I didn't even see where I was going, I was so wrapped up in my thoughts.

I'd been stunned, to say the least, to realize that I was developing *feelings* for Lily-Marie. My entire hypothesis hinged on the fact that true romantic feelings between people were bullshit. I mean, I wasn't professing to love her or anything crazy like that, but I definitely couldn't deny the feelings of attraction I'd felt when I saw her in that ball gown. It was attraction, but it had a nuance to it I couldn't describe.

Then Milly had hugged me like I raised the sun every morning and I felt something tug at my heart. Logically, I knew the heart was simply a muscle, there to pump blood and oxygen to the body and keep us alive.

And yet.

Something in my chest lurched and reformed during my time in the dressing room with those two females. My heart was pumping as usual, but it was now connected to Lily-Marie and Milly in a way I couldn't see, define, or understand. It was weird. It was disconcerting. It was nonsensical.

And don't get me started on how angry I'd become watching Lily-Marie throw herself at every male in a three-mile radius when she was having dinner with me. Okay, with me and the kids. But dammit, I wanted her attention on me, not some middle-aged loser who had no idea she dreamed of Prince Charming and sucked at sewing and forgot to put gas in her car.

Right there, standing outside my Volvo in the parking lot at Pacific Coast College, it came to me. I needed to be her Prince Charming. I needed to sweep her off her feet.

Clark told me that's who she wanted. So that's who I'd be.

I'd left a note on her car yesterday, reminding her to stop at the gas station. I'd put a flower on her doorstep the morning after our dinner thanking her for a lovely evening. All very princely actions, right?

Zero response.

It was time to pull out the items on the list of fifty ways I'd rolled my eyes at and told myself I'd never actually do.

"Aha!" I shouted. Several students walking to class eyed me

like I'd lost it, but that meant nothing to my current bubble of excitement.

I'd dance with her. And if things went really well, I'd pull her in for a swoon-worthy kiss. All of which required little to no conversation, which suited my strengths.

What could possibly go wrong?

Tuesdays and Thursdays were typically the days Lily-Marie worked from home and her car in her driveway confirmed it. I parked, exited my trusty ride, and nearly ran into my house at a full sprint. I only had an hour before she'd be leaving to pick the kids up and I needed to be properly prepared.

Wooing a woman was so far out of my wheelhouse, I was positive I'd mess it up, but I was holding out hope she'd see past my fumbles to the feelings—*shudder*—that lay beyond. Preparation was key, that I knew. So, I sprayed on cologne and took off my tie and sweater nerd uniform, leaving only a button-down shirt. I brushed my teeth and grabbed my laptop, pulling up YouTube while I raced over.

"Jameson. Hi." She answered the door, but didn't automatically step back to let me in, which was odd. Usually I got a broad smile and a warm welcome. I'd become used to that, so the opposite felt like a splash of cold water to the face.

I blinked. "Oh, I'm sorry. Am I interrupting?" What an idiot. I hadn't even thought about the fact she was supposed to be working and maybe my presence would be an intrusion.

Her cheeks went red and she smiled shyly, looking at the ground. "No, no. Come on in."

She finally stepped back and I squeezed past, purposely brushing against her ever so slightly, using my wide screen laptop getting through the doorway as the reason for stepping so close. I heard her sharp intake of breath and smiled. I was no expert, but that seemed like a very excellent thing. If she felt nothing for me, she would've breathed normally when I came close.

Either that or she feared me.

Well, that wasn't good. Maybe the gulp meant I'd intimidated her in some way, which was never my intention.

Here I was, adrift without a paddle, hoping to sweep a woman off her feet with a wish and a laptop. A serious case of wooer's remorse flooded my system as she shut the door and followed me into the living room. "Abort, abort!" were the only words racing through my brain. My mind scrambled to come up with a plausible reason for being here, if not for my original plan.

"Jameson? What's going on?"

I blinked rapidly, like that movement might stir up an idea from the sludge covering the synapsis in my brain. Lily-Marie was looking at me like I'd well and truly lost it, which perhaps I had.

What was that phrase? In for a penny, in for a pound? I was in for a tonnage. Go big or go home. That was another applicable phrase, considering home was right next door. Go for broke. I could have kept going with the maniacal idiom word play, but Lily-Marie's face was changing expression with each passing second of silence, like a human stop watch, chronicling my epic meltdown.

"Um. Well. Could you help me with my computer?" I held out my life line, the ancient but trusty computer I should have traded in years ago.

She glanced down at it and took it, even though she looked thoroughly confused. That would make two of us, sweetheart. She immediately set it on the coffee table, which was probably a good idea considering it weighed more than most hybrid cars these days.

Running her fingers over the track pad, the screen came to life. A music video from YouTube was right there on the screen.

"What seems to be the problem?" She squinted, reading the name of the song I had pulled up. "Once Upon a Dream," of course. The perfect song to melt her heart.

"I, um, couldn't get the song to play." I tugged at my shirt collar. I was winging it here and doing it poorly, I could tell.

She clicked on the video and it instantly began to play, full volume on the ginormous speakers on the sides of my laptop. "Did you try hitting the play button?" she shouted over the song.

There was no acceptable answer for that question, so I ignored it in favor of wondering what in the hell was playing. That didn't sound at all like I imagined Disney princess movies to sound like. It had a dark and slow beat. A voice began to sing that should win a year's supply of cigarettes for the throaty sexiness.

I came closer to Lily-Marie to stare at the screen. "That's 'Once Upon a Dream'?" I shouted back, even though we were mere inches apart.

When she didn't answer, I swiveled my head, seeing her gaze on my chin. I swiped, wondering if I missed some toothpaste in my hurry to get over here.

A lazy smile tilted her lips and her gaze finally lifted to mine. "Yeah. It's the Lana Del Rey version." She'd whispered this time, but I'd heard her since she'd leaned closer. So much closer. Close enough I could see her eyes dilate and the blue irises turn a deeper blue. Like staring into the ocean and wondering how deep it went.

Then she lifted her nose in the air by my neck, as if to sniff me. I had no idea what that meant or why she would smell me, but if the rosy color of her cheeks was any indicator, she could sniff me all she liked. I was definitely pro-sniffing.

"Dance with me."

Oh hell, that was me. I'd whispered that, lost in the same spell Lily-Marie appeared to be in. I hadn't even asked, just demanded, the words slipping past my lips and into the air, oblivious to my earlier command to abort the mission.

Her gaze sharpened while her body froze. I waited, frozen as well, wondering how badly I'd messed things up between us. The air felt thick, like a sudden ocean fog had come through the house, cocooning us in a world where only she and I existed. I'd never been in a fog bank with a beautiful woman, but suddenly the idea of dancing right through it seemed like the very rightest thing to do. So I did.

Without waiting for confirmation, I slid my hand around her waist and picked up her hand, assuming a formal position. When her stunned expression slid into a shy smile, I pulled her in tight, making sure there was nothing formal about this dance. The singer crooned on and I felt in that moment I'd never known anyone better.

I swayed once, she followed, her body rubbing against mine in an innocently seductive manner. The swaying kept going, fueled by a wish for more rubbing, more pressing, more time spent with her in my arms. Our gazes stayed locked together, as if blinking would break this foggy spell. Something neither of us wanted.

The song spoke of dreams, of love, of knowing someone so well it felt like a dream. She sang of everything pumping through my heart with each exaggerated beat. Everything that didn't make sense to my brain.

With sudden clarity, I knew exactly what I felt. It had taken a throaty princess song to spell it out for me.

I loved Lily-Marie.

In life, there were those things that were believed without thought or speculation. When I heard an ocean wave hit the sand for the first time I knew that sound was the most beautiful and calming sound in the world. It struck a chord somewhere in my soul. The truthfulness of it was obvious.

That's what this moment with Lily-Marie was all about. It was my brain allowing the rest of me to get a say in the matter. My soul remembered. My soul knew. And now my brain just had to catch up.

"Lily-Marie..." I breathed her name, watching her eyes melt with each deliciously slow sway back and forth.

I brought her hand to my chest, laying it there so I could push a lock of hair behind her shoulder. One touch wasn't nearly enough, so I traced the beating vein in her neck to the jawline that fit in the palm of my hand perfectly. She leaned her head into my hand, eyes nearly closing like a cat rubbing against heaven. She was warm, supple, soft. Smelling of lemons and something I couldn't describe, she was the exact combination to make me want to crawl inside her and stay forever. A safe port to weather any storm.

Desire, the likes of which I'd never experienced, rocked through my body like a lightning strike. Every cell in my body was charged, alive like never before. Lily-Marie opened her eyes, her gaze traveling up through her lashes, the look so innocent and feminine I felt a thousand feet taller. A million times more the man than I'd been before I stepped through her door.

Be courageous, not a sissy.

Give swoon-worthy movie kisses.

All signs pointed to this being our moment. My hands traced along her body, delighting in every curve she possessed, singing silent praises to her mother and father for creating such a divine creature. Then I swayed right and used the momentum to tip her over my arm, her long hair nearly dipping down low enough to sweep the floor. Her eyes widened right before a delighted cry left her mouth. I wanted to touch, to run a finger down the length of her, to see if that creamy white skin was as soft as it looked. I'd never dipped a woman over my arm, never indulged in something as romantic as this dance we found ourselves in. I paused for a moment, just taking her in, the joy and surprise and wonderment lighting up inside of me.

Before she could panic, I tilted her back upright, my hand slipping underneath the heavy fall of her hair, caressing the nape of her neck to finally grab ahold of a fistful of strands. Gently, yet firmly, I pulled her head back and claimed her lips with mine.

Rational thought fled, so instead I chased the feelings shooting through my body from our intimate point of contact. She joined the chase, an active participant to a kiss far more epic than I could have ever imagined. The minute I flicked my tongue past her lips to taste her, a dark forest flashed through my head, confusing me with its clarity. For a split second I thought we were amongst the trees instead of in her living room.

The response of her tongue, reaching out to taste me too, pushed out all thoughts of seductive forests. The heady feeling of knowing she was as into this kiss as I was spurred me on, made me pull her tighter. Her curves pressed against me, squeezed and caressed by my traveling hands. My body was strung tight, just one huge ball of pent-up desire, needing to taste and devour.

The kiss, the desperate groping, went on for what could have been hours or minutes, neither of us aware of time or space or anything so mundane besides the two of us. I had suspected she'd be like this: all feminine passion, a modern siren pulling me in and never letting me go. I could happily stay right there indefinitely, taking my sustenance from her and her alone.

Her hands suddenly squeezed my ass, hard, the shock of her bold move pulling my lips from hers momentarily. I'd never had a woman grab my ass before. There was nothing hesitant about it. Just a full-on grope that ratcheted up my desire for this incredible woman. It was playful, it was wild, it was perfect.

Then her hands were moving again and I brought her lips back to mine. A sharp tug split us apart a moment later as the top button of my shirt flew to the side. She'd ripped my shirt. I looked at her in shock, loving her aggression, yes, but also a little nervous. She giggled, her lips red and swollen. From me.

"I can fix that, I swear," she gasped, then went back to tugging on my shirt, two more buttons pinging off to hit the floor.

Her intent was clear. She wanted to destroy my shirt.

She wanted me naked.

13

ily-Marie

Oh, he was good.

The song? The dancing? The kiss?

It was like Jameson was inside my mind, experiencing the same dream that still played through my head even days later. How else could he have come over playing the same damn song from the same movie I'd been stuck in? Only the supercharged sexy version. Like he was enchanted too and couldn't wait another minute to make it real.

I'd been horrified and embarrassed to wake up and realize I'd had a sex dream about my neighbor. A really good one too. One doesn't just wake up from a dream in the middle of a real-life orgasm unless it had been one hell of a dream.

Jameson was my Prince Charming?

No way. He barely got his nose out of his textbooks long enough to observe the outside world. There was no way he knew how to sweep a woman off her feet. Well, that's what I thought until he'd shown up at my door with a proverbial boombox and played my favorite song, looking better than any scientist should with his dark frown and dress shirt open to show off just the barest hint of strong chest, a sprinkling of hair I wanted to see again. This time without my children to witness the striptease.

The beat of the song, the way he just pulled me in and took control lit a fire in my belly I'd observed in the movies but had never personally experienced. I'd been intrigued when he acted jealous at the restaurant the other night. Quite playful actually, seeing how I could push his buttons and get him to intervene. But this? This display was something else entirely.

He fisted my hair and tilted my head back, my lips served on a platter for him to take as he wished. And take he did. There was no tentative nibbling or testing, just a thorough devouring that heated my blood and warmed not just my cheeks. Little shocks of electricity shot through my body, making my muscles spasm. He held me so close I didn't fear falling, even after that dip that nearly took me to the ground.

This was like no kiss I'd ever been a part of. The crazy part was that it was better than the kiss in my dream. He was here, right below my fingertips, the press of his body begging me to join in.

My hands slid down his back, enjoying the girth of his shoulders and the line of muscles that ran down his spine to his trim waist. Then I found even greener pastures: the tight butt I'd seen in those tight bicycle shorts. Before I could think it through, I grabbed as much as I could and squeezed. He was shocked, slipping his mouth from mine with a quick intake of breath, and quite frankly, so was I. I don't recall ever groping a man's ass before, but hey, I'd never laid my eyes, or hands, on Jameson's. I wasn't sorry. In fact, I was planning to do it again.

But that break from his lips gave my eyes a chance to take in that triangle of skin above his shirt. My hands were redirected.

Before I could think better of it, the first button popped off his shirt, flying who the hell knew where. I learned exactly what force was necessary to rip a man's shirt from his body. I tucked that information into the back of my brain, secretly thrilled with myself. Jameson also seemed thrilled if the hard line digging into my stomach was any indication. His eyes looked a little skittish, but with each button that tore off, the line grew and hardened, quite like Pinocchio's nose. Part of me wanted to keep going just to see when this little growth spurt would stop. But alas, Jameson was out of buttons.

The Promised Land was before me and I didn't hesitate to jump right in. Fisting the material in my hands, I pulled his shirt off his shoulders and down his arms, frustrated by the cuffs that kept his shirt from revealing his entire upper body to me. The song ended, but we didn't care, too into each other to bother with a soundtrack.

He let me go, unbuttoning the cuffs and tossing the shirt aside, but still he towered over me, his stare pinning me in place. He didn't need to stare me down. I wasn't going anywhere. I had muscles to feel and veins to trace. There could be a five-alarm fire in my kitchen with those hot firemen coming to save me and I still wouldn't have stepped away from Jameson's hot body.

"You have a lot of sewing to do," Jameson muttered under his breath.

My hands slid their way up his flat stomach, doing another quick count of each ab muscle, then across his chest and up to his shoulders.

"Don't care. Kiss me."

His hands came back around to my backside and he lifted me off the ground like I weighed nothing. His lips crashed back onto mine and I was transported to another place, where Prince Charming took his princess and made her his. I wrapped my legs around his waist and held on tight.

When my back hit a hard surface, I fluttered my eyes open,

confused, wondering if I was back in my dream and flat against a tree. My living room came into view, my body pressed between Jameson's and the wall, the one I'd painted just last year a lovely light gray.

"Drywall is so much better than bark," I whispered against his lips.

He kissed his way down my neck. Between kisses and nips he asked, "What are you talking about?"

My entire head was about to lift off my neck from the pleasure coursing through my body. With nowhere to retreat, his cock was straining against his pants and putting pressure between my open legs, right where I desperately wanted him. A gasp escaped my mouth at the realization this was my exact dream, coming to life in suburbia.

His hips shifted and I struggled to breathe. His mouth was back, nibbling on my lip. His hands cupped my breasts, the tips of which brushed against his chest, adding to the fire that built inside of me. He was everywhere, yet I craved more.

"More, more..." I chanted in my head. I knew where this went. My dream outlined what came next.

Right on cue, he pulled the strap of my dress off my shoulder and tugged the material down, exposing the left side of my bra. I cursed my inability to plan ahead and wear my sexy bra. The one that was all lace and itchy skin irritation, yet perfectly ready for dates that never actually saw it. The standard tan satin one that had seen better days would have to do. Didn't seem to slow Jameson down. He didn't give it more than a passing glance before that too was tugged down. His head dipped and he latched onto my nipple, the tugging continuing, all the way to where he ground against my panties.

Pinned between him and the wall, all I could do was hold on to his shoulders and enjoy the ride. His hips kept rocking into my core, his cock finding the perfect spot. His tongue kept flicking my nipple, and if he just kept going for a minute or two longer, I'd orgasm with a man for the first time in years.

I closed my eyes and went to the forest, where my prince was about to drop his pants and impale me. Goddamn, that was hot. Quick breaths puffed out my mouth. I was so close.

"Mmm...Phillip."

Everything stopped.

"No, no. Keep going. Please." This wasn't how the dream went. I should be hearing a belt buckle hit the floor any second now.

Instead, I opened my eyes to Jameson staring at me wide-eyed. His hair was in a sexy disarray, probably from my fingers, though I didn't recall grabbing him. A muscle ticked in his jaw and I stared at it, stunned and confused. Where was I? More importantly, where was my orgasm?

"It's Jameson." He spoke loudly, his voice harder than what had stopped rocking against me just a few seconds too early.

My lungs constricted like I'd run a 5k, or even just a mile, who was I kidding? I shook my head. "I know you're Jameson. Why'd you stop?"

He pulled back and I locked my legs tighter around his waist. He gave me a look, one I'd seen him give Stein a thousand times. But I wasn't a naughty eight-year-old. I was a thirty-two-year-old single mom who wanted her orgasm, goddammit. He pulled back again, a little harder this time. I gritted my teeth and held on, determination my middle name. My back slid down the wall the more he stepped back.

And then I was sliding too fast, the back of my head the only thing still in contact with the wall. Jameson's worried face was above me, trying to keep me from falling, but he could barely move, what with my legs around his waist. My neck screamed at me and I finally stopped my descent only to be bent backward with Jameson above me, one hand under my back and one hand against the wall to hold us both up.

"Fuck, Lily-Marie. Let go." He barked the order that time and shit if I knew what was wrong with me, but I couldn't help the shiver that traced up my spine. Where did Jameson go and who was the commanding Don Juan in his place?

"Okay, but I go in protest." Yes, that's right. I was a girl who liked to have the last word. But I obeyed, unlocking my ankles and sliding my legs down to the ground.

He pulled us both up and I circled my head, trying to relieve my aching neck.

His gaze was fierce, perfectly complementing the ripped torso that was pumping air in and out of its lungs in greedy gulps. His dress pants stretched tight over the bulge in his pants that remained. So that wasn't the problem. He clearly wanted me.

"Why?" I whispered out loud.

He swiped a hand through his hair and looked away for a moment. His gaze lowered to my chest and I was suddenly aware that my breast was still out, valiantly trying to point at him, but mostly pointing at the ground, which seemed wildly inappropriate at the moment. I remembered quickly I was a mom of two children and things didn't look the way they had when I was twenty. Hadn't seemed to matter in the heat of things, but now in the cold light of day, I didn't really feel all that confident. Reaching up, I tucked her back in and straightened my dress with all the bravado I could muster.

When I was done, he looked me in the eye and answered me. "I wasn't going to give you an orgasm while you called me by another man's name. Was that your ex? Phillip?"

I was stunned. Phillip? When had I said that name? I sure as shit hadn't been thinking of my ex, that was for damn sure. My cheeks flamed when I realized I'd been caught between reality and my dream. For a moment there I must have said Phillip's name. Prince Phillip. From *Sleeping Beauty*.

I dropped my head to hide my smile, confident Jameson would not appreciate my mirth right now. When I had my facial muscles under control, I looked back up.

"No. That's not my ex's name, nor any man I've ever been with. I promise." I swallowed, hoping he'd believe me. Without me having to explain my sex dream.

He held my gaze for a moment and then scooped his shirt off the ground. He didn't look at me again while he put it on. "Okay."

A weight landed on my chest and I couldn't let him leave like this. I was orgasmless, but I wasn't heartless. I stepped toward him and put my hand on his arm.

"Wait, Jameson. It's not what you think. Can I be honest with you?" My heart beat wildly, realization dawning that I was getting ready to spill a long-held secret. No one else knew the extent of my obsession with movie princesses except Gabby, and even she didn't know about my sexy dream. My obsession seemed juvenile and ridiculous, but I couldn't let him walk away upset with me. Or think that make-out session wasn't as monumental to me as it really was.

He huffed out a breath. "I always want you to be honest with me." His gaze lifted from my hand on his arm to my eyes. A small win, but I'd take it, letting it bolster my confidence enough to spill my guts.

"Well, you may regret saying that when you hear this." I chuckled nervously. He didn't lose the frown, but he did nod slightly, so I took that as another good sign. "So, I have this obsession. I love Disney princess movies."

"Yeah, I know."

I froze. Was he actually inside my dream? I'd only been joking —sort of—when I'd questioned if he'd been part of my dream. Was that even possible? Who was I kidding? That was not at all in the realm of believability. Right?

"Wait. How do you know?"

"Clark told me." His classic frown was back and I resisted the urge to reach out and smooth his eyebrows. Relief flooded me and I chastised myself for being ridiculous and thinking he'd actually been a part of my dream. That was impossible, Lil, get a grip.

"Okay, so you know. Um, well, the other night I was watching *Sleeping Beauty* before bed and I must have had the movie stuck in my head because I dreamed I was in the movie that night. But it wasn't the Disney version. It was a really dirty, erotic version. And I may have, you know, said Phillip, the prince's name instead of yours because what you were doing was exactly like my dream and I just kind of lost my head there for a second." I twisted my hands nervously and found my gaze on one of the missing buttons on the floor from the front of his shirt by the time I got done spitting all that out. I couldn't look at him, wouldn't look at him, until my shame melted away enough for eye contact. So, like in maybe twenty years or so.

"Lily-Marie?" Jameson's voice held all manner of expression in its tone. Intimacy, mixed with humor, coated with relief and what I hoped was still desire. "Look at me."

I must have still been in the dream, where I would do anything my prince asked of me, because I instantly followed his instruction, finding a blazing smile on his face I'd never been blessed to see before. I was so used to his perpetual frown, the smile took me by surprise. His eyes wrinkled at the corners and the upturn of his lips softened his look, making me want to jump back on him and taste those lips again.

"Thank you for telling me." He stepped closer, his shirt flaps still open since he had no buttons left. I could feel the heat of him from several inches away.

The list of fifty ways to find a husband was never supposed to be used on Jameson, but I couldn't help but think of one of the ways I'd written out applied here far more than anything else I'd tried. "You know that's totally our song now, right?"

"Our song?" He cocked his head to the side.

"Yeah. 'Once Upon a Dream.' Don't worry, I'll play it on repeat ad nauseum until you know the words by heart." Then I realized the implication of declaring that our song. Like we were an actual couple. One interrupted make-out session did not a relationship make. "Not that we're a couple or anything. Just that the song will remind me of that wall over there and how sturdy it is."

The smile was gone, replaced by the frown, and I wondered what I'd said that irritated him so much.

14

ameson

Our song.

She said that's our song now. I couldn't be more stoked to hear her admit that we had a song. That we had a moment. That we had a connection. I honestly didn't think the fifty ways would ever work, but it did. Exponentially. Lily-Marie practically confessed her feelings right then.

I couldn't wait to get back to my journal and document how I was feeling. The energy pumping through my veins while I stood there watching my woman trust me enough to confess her deepest secrets with me was indescribable. I had to document it so I could explain it to Stein. Her hair was a mess from my hands grabbing and pulling. Her lips glowed bright red and there was razor burn on her pale neck. She'd had her legs around my waist, grinding against me without a single inhibition, and she'd been close to coming, I could feel it in the way she trembled.

But then she'd said Phillip and I'd freaked out. I couldn't have that moment with her and share it with some other man's memory. When she screamed, I wanted it to be *my* name, not some asshole before me. Of course she'd been with other men. She was a thirty-two-year-old mother, for Christ's sake, but I didn't want to hear their names when my cock was getting her off and I didn't think that was too much to ask.

The fact she'd had an erotic dream only made her even more perfect. She'd been so responsive, so out of control for me she'd ripped my shirt and tugged on my hair to the point of pain. I already knew she was sweet and funny and capable, but add in the sex siren and she was every man's wet dream.

"Not that we're a couple or anything. Just that the song will remind me of that wall over there and how sturdy it is."

Oh, hell no. We were most certainly a couple and I wanted to get that straight right freaking now.

I towered over her, needing her close to me, needing her to feel what I felt. To know what I knew. Her hands landed on my bare stomach, beneath the open sides of my shirt. My hands found her hips and pulled her in tight. I wanted her so badly, but I needed to tell her even more.

"Yes, we are a couple." I gave her a quick tug, like I could shake some sense into her. "I love you."

Her eyes widened almost comically. Had I not been in the middle of putting my heart on the line, I would have found it funny how quickly the desire faded from her eyes and fear took its place. She looked like a scared animal, looking for the quickest escape route.

My heart, so recently uncovered and cleared of dust from lack of use, took a deep dive, landing with a thud I was sure would leave bruises. She pushed against my stomach and I let her go. If she needed some space to think things through, I could understand that. It came as quite a revelation to me as well.

"Jameson." She stepped back one foot at a time until she hit the wall. The wall she'd been up against, ravenous for me, just moments before. She shook her head slowly, the scared look morphing into almost terror.

While I thought the reaction was a little over the top, I was too elated to have discovered love to be real to worry too much about what she might be thinking. For my entire thirty-four years of life, I'd operated under the belief that romantic love didn't exist. Together with Lily-Marie, I'd found out the truth: love did in fact exist and I was a lucky enough bastard to experience it. That kind of discovery was monumental. Not perhaps in science journals or academia, but in my own personal life, it was extraordinary.

"It's like I've just discovered Santa is real," I said out loud. I wasn't even sure who I was talking to, but it needed to be said.

"What?" Lily wrinkled her nose at me, which was hard to see since she was all the way across the room now, basically as far away from me as she could be while still being in the same room.

I took one step toward her. "Lil—"

"Oh gosh, look at the time. I gotta go pick up the kids." Lily-Marie looked at her wrist, which I saw didn't even have a watch on it, and she hustled around me, giving me a wide berth, chattering a mile a minute. "Don't want to be late and freak the kids out. I'll just grab my keys and be right back. Don't wait for me, I'll make sure Stein gets into your house all right."

She practically ran through the house, grabbing her purse and yanking the front door open. I stood there watching her, wondering why she was freaking out. She was clearly in the middle of a full-on freak-out, right? The common response to someone telling you they loved you wasn't to run away, was it?

"Lily-Marie," I called out. "You going barefoot?" I looked down at her feet, straddling the threshold like she couldn't wait any longer to get out of there. To get away from me. The realization of her reaction finally penetrated my glee. And fuck, did that hurt. Like a dagger straight through the chest.

She stared at her feet too, then lifted her head with a huge, plastic smile. "Oh jeez. Nope, need shoes." She ran back in just long enough to slip into some flip-flops by the breakfast table and then she was back out the door, leaving me alone in her house. Not even a "goodbye" or "hey, don't forget to lock up."

"But I did all the things on the list!" I shouted to the closed door.

I sank onto her couch and buried my head in my hands. Well, that went real smooth. I found out that love existed and I wanted to shout it from the rooftops. However, the person responsible for the revelation wanted nothing to do with me. No wonder people wrote shitty songs and poems about broken hearts. This love stuff was hard. Confusing. And it didn't even feel that good.

What was the point of making people feel ecstatic when love was predicated on a specific someone loving you back? That was bullshit! Something that awesome shouldn't depend on someone else. What if no one ever loved me back? Was I supposed to go through life just feeling like shit?

I'd rather go back to not believing in love and not getting my heart trampled on.

I sat back, slouched on the couch, feeling like I was operating under a lead weight. A black cloud. A vise squeezing my chest and reminding me of how stupid I was for loving the wrong person. Or loving at all.

Absentmindedly, I took in her living room. I'd been in her house many times before, but I realized I'd always been so focused on Lily-Marie I hadn't really looked around at her space. Her television sat on a stand against the wall opposite the couch I sat on, the cupboard below it crammed with what looked like thousands of DVDs, all bearing Disney titles. Not one romcom or thriller or sci-fi movie could be found in her collection. "Obsessed" might be too mild of a word for whatever Lily-Marie had going on here.

A framed picture of her and her children posing with Snow

White at Disneyland was on top of the DVD stand, clearly a prized possession by the way it was positioned. A pang of longing hit me full force as I stood up and walked over to examine Lily-Marie's beaming smile next to the princess. She looked more giddy than her kids.

Clark was rolling his eyes in the picture, but you could see his mouth giving way to a smile. Milly was grinning from ear to ear and holding tight to her mom's hand. I could just be projecting, but it really seemed like there was a hole in the assembly. A hole that could be perfectly filled by Stein and me.

I put the picture down and stepped away. There would be no Disneyland trips in my future if I didn't regroup and find a way to get through to Lily-Marie. I just didn't understand how she couldn't see how good we could be together. How right we were for each other.

Time to go back home and figure this thing out. Lily-Marie was it. I was sure of it.

ily-Marie

What the ever-loving hell was that? My mind was screaming the entire time I fled my own damn house. I felt like I was on the run, a fugitive who needed to escape before the cops showed up. Fleeing was essential. Fleeing was the only thing I could think of to get out of whatever that was back there.

I slammed my car door shut and put it in reverse, leaving some tread on my driveway in my haste. My lungs were burning, probably wondering why we were getting all this exercise all of a sudden. Jameson had my heart rate soaring left and right. First, he nearly nailed me against the wall in a dominant move that revved my engine just fine, and then the next he was shocking the hell out of me by professing to love me.

I repeat, what the hell was that?

Who kisses with a woman for the first time and then tells her he loves her? Okay, fine, I did that a few times in high school, literally thinking we were engaged to be married and planning our kids' names. But that was high school. Nobody was that naive by the time they hit twenty, let alone thirty.

Pulling into the school parking lot, I slammed the brakes and put the car in park. That last thought was a bit sobering, the balm I needed to calm myself. Why would Jameson react that way? Could he have so little experience with love that he was mistaking intense tonsil hockey with feelings beyond "harder, faster, oh yeah, right there?"

He had a child. I assumed he was in love with his ex-wife at some point in order to have made Stein. Although we'd never talked about our exes. For all I knew, Stein was the product of a drunken night at college. Maybe Jameson had no idea what love was about.

We barely knew each other. There was no way he could be in love with me.

I took a deep breath and felt better already. It was just a misunderstanding. I just needed to calmly tell him that he was mistaken. Things would be fine. Everything would go back to normal and it wouldn't be at all awkward living next to each other.

I heard the bell ring and kids started flooding out the doors, racing across the playground. Trying to identify my own amongst the throng was impossible. It was too bad Jameson took things way too far with his little declaration. I would have kind of liked to have a neighbor with benefits. How convenient would that have been? Kids were off to school, I worked from home two days a week. We could have had a regular sex schedule.

My vibrator was nice, definitely got the job done. But to feel a man's rough skin? To be touched and caressed by big hands, a solid weight pressing into me, pinning me against the wall? That hard cock doing unspeakable things even under layers of clothes? A shiver ran down my body.

The back door of my car opened with a loud click, disrupting my dirty thoughts and nearly giving me a heart attack. Clark hopped in, oblivious to where his mom had gone in her head. There I was, in the school parking lot, daydreaming about my neighbor's thick cock, getting all hot and bothered. I really needed that orgasm, dammit. I would have been a better mom if I'd gotten it, I just knew it. Yep, I devolved into blaming my parenting on Jameson's lack of follow-through. Seemed reasonable enough.

"How was your day, kiddo?" I eyed him in the rearview mirror, pressing my cold hands to my red cheeks, trying to calm them down and get focused.

"Good."

"Wow, what a ringing endorsement." Typical eight-year-old response. I rolled my eyes, but he was too busy getting his backpack off and buckling up to notice. "Where's Stein and Milly?"

"Milly started crying because she left her folder in the classroom. Stein went back with her to get it."

My heart melted. "Well, that was sure nice of him." You were nice to my kid? You were my new favorite person.

"He's always doing stuff like that. Drives me crazy. Like at recess today, we were in this long line to play tetherball and some kid got hit in the face. Instead of stepping up to play with me now that they were out, he took the kid to the nurse's office and we lost our turn." Now it was Clark rolling his eyes. I wondered where he got that.

"Well, honey, that was the right thing to do. Maybe next time you should follow Stein's lead, huh?"

A long suffering sigh. "I guess, Mom."

Milly and Stein opened the car doors and slid in next to Clark. I fired up the engine and headed home, listening to their chatter and banter about their day. Eavesdropping seemed like the only way to hear about what happened at school each day. When I asked, all I got was a one-word answer.

As we got closer to home, I got more and more nervous about

how to handle Jameson. I had to remember that my ultimate goal was to find a man to be a loving husband and father. I had already settled for a man who liked me, but was never in love with me. Not wanting to get married should have been a huge red flag, but of course, in the middle of desperately wanting companionship and motherhood, I'd settled for less just to keep him in my life. Of course, that only lasted until he found someone younger and more beautiful to rock his world. I wasn't still bitter, but I absolutely was focused on getting everything I wanted in a relationship next time around.

It was outrageous love or nothing, baby.

I parked the car in my driveway and eyed my house warily. Jameson was nowhere to be found. The kids hopped out and Stein ran over to his place, entering the unlocked front door. Getting out of the car, I locked it and slowly walked into my place, assuming Jameson would be gone, but not knowing for sure.

The kids raced upstairs to their rooms and my living room was blessedly empty. I couldn't help but eye the far wall, remembering what had taken place there just an hour or so ago, like the walls could talk and spill my secret.

My phone rang in my purse, startling me.

"Bejeezus, you're jumpy today, Lil," I muttered to myself.

I answered as soon as I saw it was Gabby. She was exactly who I needed to talk to.

"I need more juicy details, woman!"

"Well, hello to you too." I set my purse on the breakfast table and sank down onto the couch, kicking my flips off and getting comfortable.

"Come on now. Readers are chomping at the bit for more Mom-Com action." Gabby seemed way more excited over writing about my life than I was about living it.

"Mom-Com?" I scrubbed a hand over my forehead.

"Okay, seriously, you haven't been reading my column? What kind of best friend are you?" Gabby scoffed.

"Sorry, been a little busy living my life over here, providing you with content for your precious column." I just couldn't take the teasing, letting my snark lead the way. I was too discombobulated by everything that had happened. It was like I was living in some alternate universe today where everyone lost their goddamn minds.

Gabby's voice softened. "I'm just kidding, you know that. I really appreciate you letting me write about your dating endeavors. And so do my readers. They're eating it up! The column is called The Reality of Love, Mom-Com Style. I figured if it went well, I might do more exposés on the reality of finding love in today's world. Yours is just focused on the fact that you're a single mom and most of what happens to you is quite comical, you gotta admit. In fact, the hashtag MomCom has taken off since the articles started."

I groaned. "That's great. Just great. My life is a viral comedy."

"No, it's not like that. People are *loving* you. They *are* you. They've had similar experiences and feel like you're their new best friend. I promise you're famous in a good way. And hell, I've kept it so anonymous they have no idea who you are. Because I'm not sharing the best friend status with anybody. I'm your one and only. So spill."

I was a little overwhelmed, thinking people were following my dating escapades so closely, but it was anonymous, and if shit hit the fan in my love life, I knew I could get Gabby to keep the true level of craziness out of the column.

"You'll never guess what happened today." Her quick intake of breath was the last sound she made for ten long minutes as I whispered to her my dream, the make-out session with Jameson, and then his embarrassing declaration of love. Hopefully the kids didn't overhear any of it or I was going to have some massive explaining to do. I finally wound down and waited for her feedback.

All I heard was heavy breathing.

"Gabby?"

"Sorry. Give me a minute." I could hear a big swallow over the phone and rolled my eyes at her drama. Although, I'd been pretty freaked out for a while too, so I guess I needed to give her time to come to terms with all that had happened.

"Can I just say, holy fuck, that was hot." She let out a whoop that had me pulling the phone from my ear. "First the dream, and then Jameson bringing it to life. Damn. Despite the sweaters, that man has fire in his pants, huh?"

My cheeks went up in flames again. "Bejeezus, Gabby." But yeah, I agreed with her. He was packing heat I never expected.

"Can I just say I called it?" She cackled and it was like nails on a chalkboard. "Okay, so what's the problem here? Why are you freaked out?"

"Oh, I don't know. Because he declared his undying love for me after our first kiss? Jesus, Gabby. Men don't just do that. That's not normal." I jumped up off the couch and paced my living room, making sure to stay away from the wall that held all my secrets.

"Let's back things up here a second, okay? You started this whole Fifty Ways to Find a Husband thing because you wanted a man to sweep you off your feet, right? A man who would shower you with time, attention, and unconditional love. Oh, and also be a fabulous dad to your children. You with me?"

"Yes." I was getting a weird sinking feeling in my stomach.

"So, here's this man, who happens to be well-educated and gainfully employed, so we can assume he won't pickpocket you. He understands your life as a single mom because he's a single father too. Your kids get along great. He's hotter than Chris Hemsworth and compliments you left and right while he takes you clothes shopping. When you cut yourself, he bandages your finger like he's nurturing an abandoned baby bird. He literally sweeps you off your feet to your favorite song and almost fucks you against the damn wall, but respects himself—and you—so much that he backs off when you call him by the wrong name. And then he throws himself at your feet and professes his love for you."

Silence stretched out over the phone.

My stomach was clawing at my insides. I was miserable. So miserable it felt a lot like how I'd felt when Shawn first left two years ago. I'd been adrift, stunned, confused, and hurt. Take all that and add in a layer of massive guilt and you'd feel what I was feeling right then.

"What the hell is wrong with you?" Gabby was practically shouting, making me wince.

Tears flooded my eyes and my throat swelled.

"I just—" I sniffled loudly, trying to hold back the tears. "I wasn't using the fifty ways on him and he's supposed to be my neighbor, not my love interest. And we just met. How can he love me?"

"Oh, Lil." Gabby sighed. "Who cares if you were using that stupid list on him? The point is to find a good man, not to prove this list works. I think the real reason you're having trouble with all this is because of your last question. How could Jameson be in love with you?"

I threw my hand in the air. "I don't know! That's what I'm saying. It's crazy!"

"Mhmm..."

I really freaking hated it when Gabby did that. She had something to say but wouldn't say it. But I was all out of fucks today. I wasn't playing her little game. If she didn't want to tell me, fine. But I wasn't going to sit here and play twenty questions.

"Look, I gotta go. The kids need to be doing their homework right now. Talk later?"

"For sure. Just promise me you'll think on that last question, okay?"

"Okay, sure, see ya." I hung up, feeling even worse than before she called.

I threw my phone on the couch and went to get the kids rounded up for homework time while I started dinner. And if I didn't have much of an appetite, I blamed it on my stress at work. If I was a little short with the kids, it was because they were being difficult on purpose. If I glanced out the front window constantly, it was because I thought I heard an Amazon delivery, not because I was checking to see if my neighbor was coming by to hash things out. If I went to bed and couldn't even stomach watching my favorite Disney movie for fear of another dream, it was because I was too tired to keep my eyes open.

And yet, open they stayed, into the wee hours of the morning.

When I woke, I had a plan. A new determination to finish this damn list and find a man. The list would work, Jameson was not the man of my dreams, and today I'd get to work on proving it.

~

The Reality of Love, Mom-Com Style - episode #7

We have news. Big news. Three little words, two people, and one stolen kiss. Okay, the kiss turned into a delicious make-out session against the wall involving many kisses, but that didn't go with my clever count-down. Our girl, Betty, is running scared, but you can't really outrun your next-door neighbor, can you? *Cue maniacal laugh.* Let the record state I see these two together. Like love and marriage and a baby carriage, together.

Neighbor man better step up his game and wrangle her in. He's got his work cut out for him, because if I know Betty, she's going to come back swinging with a vengeance in the form of man-hunting 1950s style on steroids.

Hang tight, dear readers. The chase is heating up!

~

I made a miscalculation.

After the third shoe turned up with teeth marks in it, I was open to the idea that this was a bad idea. I'd studied my list and picked the one that seemed the most promising for myself, and for the kids. I'd made some calls from work on Friday and I got the delivery on Sunday morning while the kids were still with their dad.

Meanwhile, I was stuck with my bad decision and wondering if I could take it back before the kids saw him. He was cute really, this new man of the house I'd gotten. All ten pounds of fur and big paws and clumsy tumbling. The golden retriever puppy looked at me with these big golden-brown eyes that melted my heart.

Until I saw my shoes. Then that mushy heart froze over a bit and the puppy eyes didn't hold so much power. The list had said to adopt a puppy and take it for walks to attract the single men. I'd researched good breeds for kids and found a shelter who had a whole litter of golden retriever puppies looking for a good home.

If nothing else, he'd provided companionship today while my kids were gone. Jameson had been nowhere to be found. Since I ran out on him Thursday afternoon, I hadn't seen him at all. It almost seemed like he was ignoring me.

Which made that layer of guilt build higher and higher until I was practically choking on it. The even sadder fact was that I realized I missed him. He'd always been coming over and helping out with the kids. He was just there, being his dorky, awkward self and making me laugh. And I hadn't even realized it. Until he wasn't.

So I kept Puppy and kept glancing out the window where I could see Jameson's driveway. I wasn't sure what I'd do if I saw him, but it seemed imperative that I actually lay eyes on him. You know, to just make sure he was among the living. For all I knew, he'd been lovestruck and then struck down, lying in a heap on the floor just waiting for a dutiful neighbor like myself to come check on him.

"Gah!" I hopped off the couch, disgusted with myself. Two days of no Jameson and I was ready to chuck my man-plan. Puppy scrambled to his feet so fast, he spun out and face-planted. That brought a smile to my face. Not him hurting himself, but just how eager he was to interact with me. Jameson might be ignoring me, but Puppy thought I was better than a squirrel up a tree.

"We need to give you a name, sweet boy." I ruffled his fur and the minute my hand left his head, he was jumping onto my shins for more. What was with puppies that made me talk in that little baby voice? "You're just so cute, aren't you? You love it when I talk to you like this, huh? Yes, you do. Good boy."

A car door slamming outside had me scrambling to my feet, looking a lot like Puppy when he tried to get up. Feet solidly under me finally, I ran to the front window, my heart about to beat out of my chest. I lifted one blind slat and peered out, hoping to see Jamison. Instead, I saw my ex climbing out of his new Mercedes.

"Well, that's a disappointment," I muttered to myself. It was enlightening to see Shawn after spending time with Jameson. The differences were startling. Shawn was smaller, shorter, and lighter complected. He'd gone soft around the middle after turning thirty, focusing on work and late-night drinks with clients, leaving no time for working out. Instead, he wore a flashy watch and drove a fancy car, the accouterments that screamed he was someone of importance.

Jameson, on the other hand, was tall and brooding, with muscles and thick hair I could still feel sliding between my fingers. Jameson didn't need expensive objects to exude confidence. It was in the way he studied things before speaking, how he observed and processed a problem with that brilliant mind of his. His confidence whispered softly in the way he treated women and children; like they were the most important people on earth, to be treasured and revered, not left at home eating dinner alone yet again.

My chest squeezed painfully, missing Jameson. The pain, sharp and deep, had me rubbing my chest as I watched my ex get the kids out of the car and walk up the driveway. I was surprised. I'd spent most of my time being annoyed with Jameson for distracting me from using all the Fifty Ways to Find a Husband, and here I was, now pining for him like a heartbroken woman. I'd been heartbroken when my ex left too, but that break also brought a breath of fresh air, like I'd dodged a bullet.

This pain? This just felt like the biggest mistake of my life.

16

ameson

"Dad! They have a dog!" Stein nearly slid past my office door in his socks. The wide eyes and loud shout gave away the level of his excitement.

I closed my laptop on top of my desk and tried to pull my brain into the conversation. I'd been in the middle of building some extra assignments into the curriculum for second quarter, but got very little done as every other thought was about Lily-Marie and what I should do about our tenuous situation.

"What's that?"

Stein ran into my office and grabbed my shoulders, his face level with mine while I sat, so earnest I bit back a smile, even in my current funk.

"Clark and Milly. They have a dog!" He grabbed my hand and pulled with all his might. I acted like he'd yanked me from my chair with a force much greater than a guy his age could muster.

"Jeez. Been working out, buddy?" I let him tug me toward the front door, where I finally planted my feet and looked out the window. I wasn't keen on the idea of going over there and seeing Lily-Marie face-to-face. She and I had unfinished business and I had zero confidence I could casually interact with her in front of the kids without dropping to my knees and begging for her to love me back.

Yeah, I know. Pathetic, right?

A cursory glance outside wasn't enough for Stein. All the sight did was stir up his excitement for all things canine. Jumping around on a bright blue leash was a floppy light-haired puppy, attached to the woman I'd been obsessing over. She, of course, looked like a ray of sunshine in that yellow dress I loved so much, her long hair curling down her back and her easy smile making me wonder if she thought of me at all.

Clark and Milly pet—mauled—the dog, getting him tangled in his leash. Several other neighbors were out, talking to Lily-Marie and meeting the puppy. All in all, it looked like they were having a nice little family afternoon with their new addition. Like my profession of love wasn't even on her mind. Like I wasn't over here dying with each minute of silence that passed.

"Can we go pet him, Dad?" Stein tugged on my arm again, doing that dance that looked like he had to pee when he was little, but was now just his "excited" dance.

My shoulders drooped. There was no way to say no. It was a goddamn puppy, for Christ's sake.

"Sure. Let's go pet the puppy."

Stein flew out the door, leaving me behind, and I was tempted to just stay there in my doorway, watching from the sidelines. I'd done a fairly good job the last few days staying away from Lily-Marie. After her sprint to get away from me, I figured she needed some space. Maybe some time to come to terms with her feelings. Maybe a full day before she came running over to tell me she loved me too. But one day turned into three and here I was afraid to leave my house for fear of having to talk to her.

A shirtless runner came down the sidewalk and made a beeline for Lily-Marie, his sweaty chest glistening in the late afternoon sun. I froze, right there on the doorstep, reduced to a lurker in the shadows. The asshole flexed his abs—so obvious—and asked her a question that had her throwing back her head in laughter. The bastard had the audacity to reach down and pet the dog, like he was part of their little family unit. Then he ran his hand through his hair, real casual, showing off his biceps like an Arnold Schwarzenegger wannabe. Unfortunately, the move also showed off his overly trimmed arm pit hair and how stupid was that? I bet he Nair'd his chest too. No man over twenty had literally zero hairs on their chest naturally.

A surge of anger flooded my averagely hairy chest and I couldn't stand around any longer. I stalked over to the group, intent on breaking up this little flirt session. Nothing wrong with reminding Lily-Marie I existed.

"Hey, Lily-Marie. You guys got a dog?" I asked, pumping a smile I didn't feel into my question.

She spun around with what I could have sworn was a look of delight before schooling her features and answering me.

"Yeah, thought the kids could use a family pet. We don't have a name for him yet, but we're going to pull names from a hat tonight and let fate pick it." She ducked her head and smiled down at the cloud of fur, currently rolling on its back and receiving belly rubs from six small hands.

I was encouraged to see her keep her back to Mr. Sweaty Chest, the guy who was currently giving me a glare I understood all too well. It was the same one I wore every time Lily-Marie pulled her flirting stunts with other men around me.

"Dad, check him out. We should totally get one too!" Stein's face nearly cracked in two with his huge smile.

Now that I was at her side, I hated to leave Lily-Marie, but the kids were there. No deep conversations could be had, and besides, I was kind of upset with her. I'd vomited my feelings to her and she'd run away. Maybe the vomit part was the problem. But how was I supposed to know love confession etiquette? Up until three days ago, I didn't believe that romantic love even existed.

So, I walked a few steps away and squatted down with the kids to pet the puppy. He was super soft and warm, lapping up all the attention. He even squeezed in a few licks on my hand, stealing my attention from Lily-Marie and her runner guy. Until he opened his big mouth, that is.

"I didn't realize you lived around here."

Damn, the second I walked away, he was back at it, flirting like he had no respect for the minors in listening range.

I glanced up and caught Lily-Marie blushing. Fuck. Right in front of me, she met a guy. He looked pretty strong, like he could totally sweep her off her feet. Just like she wanted.

"Hey, Jameson, can you help us show him how to play fetch?" Clark shoved something in my hand, a brand-new blue rubber ball, to match the dog's collar, I'd bet.

Anger burned up my esophagus, Lily-Marie's interest in other men creating the worst acid reflux known to humankind. But there were three eager kids looking at me to help them with their new four-legged family member and I couldn't let them down.

"Sure, kiddo. It's all about positive reinforcement. The leash isn't that long, so let's toss the ball to him and see if he'll pick it up at least. If he does we'll shower him with praise. Okay?" I scooted back and gestured for the kids to follow, crouching down to their level again.

Milly climbed on my back and wrapped her arms around my neck, wanting a higher vantage point for all the action. A bit of the fire burning through my system faded away at her ready acceptance. Her mother might not like me, but Milly sure did.

I tossed the ball right to the puppy and we all waited with

bated breath while he sniffed it, pawed at it, and then hopped around while it lay there inert on the ground. Meanwhile, I could hear Mr. Sweaty Chest inviting Lily-Marie to join him on his next run. I snorted at the thought. Like she'd voluntarily go running. What an idiot.

Clark glanced over at me, probably wondering why I was snorting at nothing. I just smiled back, then stood up to go get the ball. Milly squealed in my ear, enjoying the piggyback ride. We stooped and I let Milly lean over my shoulder to be the one to pick up the ball. The puppy licked her hand and she giggled, the sound bringing another smile to my face.

Hustling back over to the boys, I had Milly chuck the ball at the dog, and this time, he sniffed at it and then picked it up in his mouth. When we all burst out cheering, he looked up, startled, and dropped the ball again. At our collective groan, Lily-Marie came over to see what was going on. Thankfully, marathon boy took the hint and took off, leaving Lily-Marie blessedly alone.

"What are you guys up to?"

She stood right next to me, her hand on Milly's back, which put her breast pressed firmly against my arm. A waft of her perfume hit my nose and I nearly dropped Milly. I tried to swallow, but my throat felt too tight.

"We're gonna teach him how to play fetch, Mom," Clark explained.

I was watching the puppy, studiously ignoring Lily-Marie, but I could feel her breathing next to me. Hell, I could feel her gaze on the side of my head, her stare not leaving me once. I had no idea what she'd say to me or what she was feeling, but I couldn't look at her. Not while the kids were there. I simply didn't trust myself.

"If anyone can teach him, I'd bet on Jameson." She almost whispered it, her mouth only a foot away from my ear.

A shiver ran down my spine at her intimate tone. I kept up a steady chant, reminding myself not to look at her. Not the time, nor the place. I had more self-control than that, I knew I did.

"Hey, Lily-Marie! You got a new dog there?" Mr. Stinebeck, from down the street, called over from the sidewalk, ripping Lily-Marie's attention from the side of my head.

I winced. Good Lord, it was like the freaking *Bachelor* show around here. Every damn neighbor was a man and every single one of them wanted to talk to Lily-Marie. A flutter of something I didn't recognize threatened to consume me, even as the kids went back to playing fetch with their dog.

As I watched Lily-Marie talk with Mr. Stinebeck, his hand patting her back far too intimately for my liking, I decided enough was enough. No need to torture myself further.

Lowering Milly to the ground, I stood back up and clapped my hands. "All right, guys. I gotta start making dinner. Good luck with the puppy."

With that, I spun on my heel and marched back inside my house. Not one backward glance. An exit I could be proud of.

When I got inside and closed the front door—didn't even slam it—I proceeded to slap two cans of soup down on the counter and took my anger out on the can opener. None of that electric can opener business for me. I did it the old-fashioned way with elbow grease and anger.

By the time the soup was boiling on the stovetop, I was rapidly running out of hope. Instead of debating when Lily-Marie would come to her senses and realize she loved me, I was contemplating moving yet again. How disruptive would that be for Stein?

I let out a sigh. "Dumbass..."

I couldn't ask Stein to move again so soon. Simply because his father was an idiot and fell in love with the girl next door, too much of a nerd to figure out how to make her fall in love with him in return.

So that was it. I was destined to live out the rest of my life here in this house, watching the woman I loved flirt with everyone but me.

Unrequited love. My new friend.

Stein was in his pajamas, curled up on one end of the couch as we watched his favorite YouTube channel with two grown adults playing Minecraft and narrating their way through the adventure. He giggled when one of the narrators screamed and died a fiery death, the sound normally being enough to make even my most stressful days bright again. But even my son's giggles couldn't lighten the dark thoughts that pounded through my head.

Instead, I grabbed my journal and got busy scribbling into it while Stein was occupied. I needed to write out everything that had happened between Lily-Marie and me. The conclusion to the infamous experiment that had gone all wrong. As I wrote out how I felt watching her today, I realized I was jealous. I was wholly green with it, finally understanding that phrase for the first time.

I was so deep into my thoughts, a silent pity party for my single status, I didn't hear Stein turn off the television. Only when he placed his hand on my arm, did I put the pen down and look up.

"Did you hear me, Dad?" Stein patiently asked me. He knew how I was when I was reading, writing, or thinking. I never heard someone unless they shouted my name multiple times, too caught up in my head to be aware of my surroundings.

I blinked. "I'm sorry. What's that, son?"

"I asked you what was wrong. You're over here, like, grunting." He giggled.

I didn't blame him. My love life, and my reaction to it, was quite pathetic. One day I hoped to look back on all this and giggle too. Like, years from now. Maybe when I was in the old folks' home and half senile anyway.

"You really want to know?" I lifted an eyebrow, daring him.

He scooted closer, face earnest. "Dad, is this about Clark's mom?"

Damn these kids and their perception. They always knew what was going on, except for when it was time to do chores and they played dumb. I covered my surprise as much as I could.

"Well, it's mostly about that experiment I told you about when we first moved here."

"The one about true love?"

"Yep, that's the one. Remember how I was going to run an experiment to prove that romantic love doesn't exist?"

Stein nodded, still looking more serious than an eight-year-old should. "Yeah, I remember. Did you finish the experiment?"

I set my journal aside and shifted so I faced him. This conversation required my full attention. "I sure did. I borrowed some tactics from a magazine article and unleashed them on Lily-Marie. My hypothesis claimed she wouldn't be affected. Love wouldn't suddenly appear out of thin air, thus proving me right."

I paused, struggling for how to describe what actually happened.

"And? Did you get your hyp-thus correct?"

Sigh. "Nope, not even a little bit."

Stein gasped. "Lily-Marie is in love with you?"

I chuckled ruefully. "Nope, not even a little bit." Stein's eyebrows drew into a frown. "*I* fell in love with *her*."

Stein's face cleared and he hopped off the couch to stand in front of me. "That's great, Dad!"

I couldn't help but smile at his enthusiasm. His support was heart-melting, even if misplaced. "Well, not really. She's not in love with me, so that means I'm kinda frustrated and miserable right now."

Stein shook his head. "Nah, you're just focusing on the wrong things right now, Dad, and that's making you miserable."

"What do you mean?"

"First of all, you discovered that romantic love exists and that's fantastic news, don't you think? And second of all, you just gotta make your grand gesture and Lily-Marie will love you too. That's how they always do it in the movies." He shrugged, like everything was figured out.

"My grand gesture, huh?" I scrubbed a hand through my hair. Didn't sound any worse than what I was currently thinking about, which focused primarily on giving up. "What exactly is a grand gesture?"

"Haven't you been watching all the movies we see? The guy always makes a big plan to show the woman how much he loves her. Like in *Sleeping Beauty*, he kissed her to wake her up. In *Moana*, he sails across the earth to help her. In a *Dog's Purpose*, he travels through several lifetimes, just to bring two people in love together. A grand gesture."

Hope flares, a tiny flame about to sputter out at the slightest gust of wind. Or maybe ready to burst into a huge wall of flame with the slightest bit of encouragement from an insightful boy.

"A grand gesture," I repeated myself, the idea taking root, building and growing into something beautiful and earnest and raw. Declaring I loved Lily-Marie was only the first step to sharing myself with her, I realized. The real declaration of love wasn't in the words, but in the listening, in the doing. I needed to listen to her, fully understand what she needed in a partner, and then be that partner. Not because I needed her. But because she needed me. Because I wanted to be the man she deserved.

I grabbed my pen and opened the journal again, turning to a fresh page and leaning forward, my forehead almost touching Stein's.

"Let's get to brainstorming, son."

17

ily-Marie

I didn't know if it was being sleep-deprived from Butterscotch, the name drawn out of the hat for our new puppy, or if it was a natural function of missing the man next door. Either way, I dragged ass all week, my normal energy drained like my cell phone battery by the end of the day.

I hadn't figured out what to do about Jameson, nor had I continued my list of ways to find a husband. I was stuck, stagnant, standing in one place and getting damn sick of myself in the process. My stomach got queasy every time I thought of Jameson's face when the guy from down the street asked me to go running with him. The idea of implementing any of the other ways on my list made me want to hurl.

But I couldn't make myself go over there and talk to Jameson either.

I called myself every name in the book. It boiled down to the fact I was, in fact, a big, fat chicken. Something kept holding me back and I couldn't put my finger on it. The bouquet waiting for me every morning on my welcome mat didn't help matters either. There was never a note, but I knew they were from Jameson. It was the same bouquet of flowers he'd given me that first night I'd invited him and Stein over for dinner. His intent was clear: he wasn't done wooing me. He'd backed off substantially, but not entirely.

I loved those flowers and dreaded them at the same time. My thoughts and feelings were all over the map and there I stayed, stuck in one place, no decision of any kind made yet. So when Shawn showed up Saturday morning to take the kids for the weekend, I was in a mood more foul than any man should have to withstand.

"Back by five tomorrow?" I snapped from the front door. The kids hustled to his car, probably anxious to get away from Grumpy Mom. Shawn spun around on the front porch and eyed me warily.

"Everything okay, Lily?"

Oh, now that was brave. A mistake, but brave nonetheless for such a spineless little man.

"Oh, just great, thanks for asking." I smiled an overly sweet smile, the kind so sweet it makes you queasy. The pressure was building and I felt like it just might take me with it when it exploded. Then, like a demon possessed, I spewed forth questions, the ones I'd never asked in the two years we'd been apart. "Did you ever love me? Or were we more like a pair of ratty old slippers, comfortable and easy? Did you just keep me around until you found a brand-new shiny pair? Or did I do something to stop you from loving me?"

Shawn staggered back a step, surprised as I was by the twenty questions. Apparently, the explosion I feared looked a lot like verbal diarrhea once it spewed. We'd never really fought when we split, he just quietly gathered his things and moved out. Thoughts and feelings were never really discussed.

He glanced over his shoulder quickly, seeing the kids safely inside his car. "What's this about?" His gaze met mine and he looked properly cautious.

I slumped against the doorway, tired now that the questions were out there, hovering in the space between us. "I don't know. I just—I'm trying to understand."

Shawn stepped closer, his body rigid and prepared for flight. "You were never a pair of slippers. But I do think loving each other became habit, something we did because it was the natural progression of our dating. I just got to a point where I didn't think that was enough to keep us together. We both deserved to be passionately in love with someone else. That was the main thing. There was no passion between us. I still love you, Lily. Like I love my sister, or my best friend." I cringed, but he kept going. "I deserve more. You deserve more. You're a beautiful woman and will make someone ecstatically happy one day. It's just not me."

As harsh as that was to hear, the words rang true. Like everything in me resonated with what he said, accepted it as true, recognized it as my own truth too. I wondered why I still harbored feelings of not being enough, like our split was proof of it. That just wasn't true and I was finally able to receive the message. Ultimately, I was happy he'd had the insight and courage to end things when he did.

A rush of affection for this man, the one I should have only been friends with, flooded through my body, causing tears to blur my vision. I stepped forward and wrapped my arms around his shoulders.

"Thank you. You're so right," I whispered.

He hugged me back for a moment and then we broke apart awkwardly.

He hooked a thumb over his shoulder. "Gotta get going."

I nodded, stepping back. "See you tomorrow."

As he walked back to his car, I felt completely different than I had this morning. Or all week. Like that simple conversation with my ex had locked something into place. In the back of my mind, I'd always wondered if I just wasn't good enough to love. If maybe I just wasn't enough, period.

Our breakup hadn't been about me at all. It was about both of us equally. About two people not being right for each other. About two people being given a chance at love again. About two people being courageous and brave and daring.

Shawn, in his own way, had already done that. It may have taken me two years to get my head screwed on straight, but I was ready now. I was ready to be brave. To take a chance on love. To lay it all on the line and open my heart up to something wild and crazy and wonderful.

Something that looked a lot like Jameson.

"I'm running out of material, woman! Get your flirt on, would ya?" Gabby answered the phone without even a hello, just getting right down to business.

"I'm kind of done with that now, Gabs." I paced my living room, staring out into my backyard, my brain whirling.

"What do you mean 'done'? Did you finally give up on the list? What happened?" Gabby's voice turned soft, taking off her reporter hat and putting on her bestie hat instead.

"Nothing happened. Well, that's not accurate. Everything happened. I just talked to Shawn." I rubbed my forehead. This wasn't coming out right.

"Oh, no, honey. Don't listen to that man. He's never understood you."

"No, no. It was a really good conversation. We never loved each other, you know? I mean, we did and we still do, but not in the way a husband and wife should. We were an old pair of slippers and I want glittery ruby red slippers."

"Okaaaayyy."

I rolled my eyes. "I know I'm not making sense, but everything makes total sense in my head finally. I loved the idea of being with Shawn. Being together forever, building a home, having kids. It was everything I always wanted. Except I did it with the wrong man. He did me a favor by leaving. He gave me a chance to actually have everything I've ever wanted with the right man."

"Now you're making sense. That's essentially what I was asking you last weekend. Why are you so certain that Jameson can't possibly love you?" Gabby's voice came out fast, almost like she had the phone pressed to her face in her excitement.

I flopped onto the couch, too flabbergasted to keep my legs under me. "Oh my God, Gabriella."

"Right?"

"How could I be such an idiot?"

Gabby laughed softly. "Honey, you're not an idiot. You're just too busy watching your Disney movies to understand a fundamental truth about yourself."

My stomach started fluttering, not nauseous like I'd been all week, but excited. Like I had everything to look forward to again. "I didn't believe Jameson loved me because I thought I was unlovable. I believed that because Shawn never loved me like that, no other man could either. I'm not some beautiful princess in a fairy tale. I'm just a mom with stretch marks and cellulite and worries keeping me up at night, trying to find happiness like everybody else. But, Gabby, I'm not unlovable at all. I'm quite fucking lovable. I'm the most lovable love thing that's ever been loved. I just hadn't found the right man yet."

"Yes," Gabby whispered, then louder, "Yes!" Then much calmer, "Wait, you said that past tense. Does that mean you've found the right man now?"

The fluttering gained force, blowing off the dust from my heart, making it beat wildly, passionately. "I'm not entirely sure. Maybe. Possibly. I'll never find out for sure if I don't take a chance. He said he loves me. He's seen me in my ugly mom bra, juggling my kids, stressed about work, stumbling around trying to catch a man with my ridiculous list. If he can love me like that, he must truly love all of me, right?"

"So, are you going to wait for him to sweep you off your feet?" Gabby, the holder of my secrets for my whole life, knew me like no one else. Knew my dreams of Prince Charming coming for me. But that dream just felt old and stiff, like a shirt worn and washed too many times over the years. It was time to take it off for good. Time to find a new shirt.

"Nah, that's for fairy tales. I'm gonna go sweep him off *his* feet and see what happens." I fiddled with my sweater, nerves and excitement mixing together and bringing back every drop of energy I'd lacked all week.

"Want to help me come up with a plan?" I needed reinforcements. I couldn't afford for this to turn out like my attempts at finding a man, ending in embarrassment.

"Oh Lordy, don't tell me we're gonna make another list," Gabby grumbled.

I burst out laughing. "No! No more lists, no more ridiculous ways to meet men. I've met him already. I need a plan to make sure he knows how serious I am about us. I've ignored the man for a week and a half after he poured his heart out. I gotta make this good, so good he'll forgive me and give me another chance."

"Okay, let's think about this. He's a scientist, so we need to approach this practically."

"I could buy him another one of his precious sweaters."

"No, that's not enough. Not a big enough statement." Gabby hummed while she thought.

I snapped my fingers. "I got it! I'll write an essay on love. Every scientific fact about it, where it comes from, how we feel it, how one feels it in the body. Like proving love exists and I know that's what I feel about him."

Gabby snorted. "That's the weirdest way I've ever heard to woo a guy, but considering your particular man, I get it. Probably wouldn't hurt, but maybe just explaining everything to him would be good too. Tell him how you feel and why you ran away."

I gulped. "Yeah, honesty is probably the best policy."

I just had to quit being a chicken.

A car door slamming had me jumping up and running to the front window. Jameson's ex was back, parked at the curb and leaning against the car while she waited for Stein.

I kept snooping like the crazy neighbor I was and saw Stein, loaded with a stuffed backpack, give Jameson a big hug by their front door. Stein got a big smile on his face and then fist-pumped his dad. Jameson watched them leave before spinning around and going back in his house.

I had to hurry. A whole day without either of our kids meant I needed to write that essay right now and find the courage to face him no later than this afternoon. This conversation required privacy and the time was now. As single parents, we had a small window of childless time. I'd better use it to my fullest advantage.

Fingers trembling and heart pounding, I sat at my breakfast table with my laptop and pounded out an essay to win back my chance at love.

18

ameson

I took deep breaths to keep from puking right on my new dress shoes, the brown oxfords that complemented my new charcoal gray suit perfectly. My grand gesture was underway, no chance to turn back now, and I was straight terrified. Rejection was a distinct possibility. Humiliation would be its close cousin.

All week I'd been making phone calls and setting things in motion, all with the idea of sweeping Lily-Marie off her feet just like she'd dreamed of since she was a little girl watching a Disney princess movie for the first time. For a guy who wasn't so great with his words, I'd had frank conversations with more people than I ever cared to do again. But nothing was too much for the woman I loved. Even my own possible humiliation.

Staring at my washed-out complexion in the mirror, I heard a car outside. It was showtime.

"Here goes everything," I muttered, resisting the urge to tug at my hair. I'd just gotten it to lie down flat, I couldn't be messing it up now. If all went right, I hoped Lily-Marie would be the one to mess it up.

I ran to the front door, stopping to grab my phone and wallet. A black limousine sat idling at the curb in front of Lily-Marie's exactly as I'd asked them to do. A black-suited driver stood by the back door and if his posture and purposeful stare out into nothing was any indication, he'd been military at some point. I stopped on my front porch to shoot a text to Gabby, one of my accomplices to this grand gesture.

Me: *Limo is here. Hopefully, she'll be at the store in twenty minutes or so. You good to go?*

Gabby: *Hell yes! Let's Cinderella this girl.*

Chuckling at her enthusiasm, I jogged out to meet the driver. Gabby had assured me many times this week that Lily-Marie would participate and appreciate my plans. I hoped to God she was right.

"Hey, man, thanks for being on time. I'll be right back with your passenger. Remember, this is all a surprise, so please don't tell her anything no matter how many questions she asks, okay?"

He shook my hand and wasted no time on comforting words. "Got it."

I raised an eyebrow as I spun around and marched up to Lily-Marie's front door. I knocked and stood there with my heart in my throat. I was nervous as hell, but I also just wanted to talk to her, see her. I'd missed her like crazy.

The door cracked open and then swung all the way open. All the butterflies in my stomach left me the minute I laid eyes on her. She was in a pair of jeans and a T-shirt with Mickey ears. Her hair was piled on top of her head and she had glasses perched on her nose.

"When did you get glasses?" As soon as the question left my mouth, I wanted to smack myself. We hadn't talked in almost two weeks and that was what I led with?

She blushed and pulled them off. "A couple weeks ago. I just need them when I'm on the computer." She narrowed her eyes, a soft smile on her face. "How've you been, Jameson?"

"I've been better, honestly. I've got a surprise for you, though. Do you trust me?" I held my hand out, wondering if she'd recognize the line from *Aladdin*.

The smile grew and she put her glasses down on the entry table and took my hand, stepping closer.

"Thank you for the flowers. My house looks like a beautiful florist." Her voice lowered, like her words were just for me.

I pulled her hand to my lips and kissed her silky skin, immediately remembering how soft she was and how much I'd missed having my lips on her. Stepping to the side, I gave her a view of the limo. But she just kept staring at me, not noticing the huge vehicle in front of her house.

"Your carriage awaits, m'lady." I swooped my hand out to the curb and she finally looked away, just then noticing the limo and the driver.

"Wha—" Her mouth dropped open and I silently sent up a prayer she'd go along with the plan.

"You have an appointment and I made sure you had an appropriate ride to get you there." The whole time I spoke, I walked her out to the curb, stopping in front of the driver, who held the back door open for her.

"But—wait. Jameson." She gripped my hand tight and turned to me, her back to the limo. "Jameson, I want to talk to you."

I pulled her close and kissed her cheek. "I know. I promise we'll talk after. But you can't be late. See you in a little bit."

Like in a trance, Lily-Marie stepped to the open door and I helped her in. She wasn't smiling, but she was going along with it and that was all I needed right then.

Unable to help myself, I leaned in and kissed her quickly, her hands coming up to reach for me. I ducked out of the way, regretting it, but knowing it was for the best. I had to pace this date.

The driver slammed the door shut and I stepped back onto the curb.

Watching the limo take off down the street, I let hope fill my chest, bringing a smile to my face. For the first time in almost two weeks, I felt like things were on the right track. That we could make this work.

When the limo turned the corner, I pulled out my phone and texted Gabby again to let her know Lily-Marie was on her way to her. Then I pocketed my phone and hustled back to shut Lily-Marie's door and then back to my house to continue pulling strings and orchestrating this date.

Four hours later, the limo made its way back down our street. Thankfully, I'd had rushed texts from Gabby all afternoon to keep me from losing my mind. The dress fitting had gone perfectly, with Lily-Marie walking out in the dress she'd tried on when we'd gone clothes shopping with the kids. I couldn't wait to see her in the turquoise ball gown, the one that highlighted every curve she owned like a boss.

I'd made a mad dash to the store with Lily-Marie's purse and cell phone to hand off to Gabby. I knew she'd want it in case the kids called. They too knew about the plan for today. I'd told them yesterday when they were in the backyard playing with Butterscotch. I pinkie promised them to keep it a secret, and miraculously, they had. Lastly, I ran Butterscotch over to Gabby's house, praying he didn't chew up all her furniture before she got home.

Lily-Marie made it to her hair and makeup appointment right on time, thanks to Gabby rushing her along. I just hoped Gabby had been able to stick to her guns and not let out the secret. She'd sworn to me she'd keep everything to herself, but I knew how persuasive Lily-Marie could be. Four hours was a long time to keep this big of a secret from your best friend.

The limo came to a stop and that puke-y feeling was back. I opened the back door before the driver could get there, too excited and nervous to wait. The next step of this grand gesture was ready, I just needed my date.

A silver strappy stiletto emerged first, then the gorgeous curvaceous leg it was attached to, the one that had been wrapped around my waist not long ago. Then a flash of turquoise and finally, Lily-Marie's beaming face.

"Jameson." She looked stunned. Her expression was entirely different than the stunned look she'd had running away from me when I told her I loved her. I wasn't sure why this time was different, but I'd spend all night convincing her how good we could be together so she never ran away again. My words would not fail me this time.

I held out my hand and she accepted, standing up out of the limo, her lush breasts brushing against my chest. Somehow, I'd forgotten how perfect that dress was for her, highlighting her many assets. I just hoped I was the lucky man who got to spend eternity with her.

"Are you hungry?" I took in her features, the smoky eyes, the lush lips with some kind of unnecessary gloss on them. Her hair was piled on top of her head still, this time with pins and curls artfully arranging her long locks. She was stunning.

"Starved," she whispered back, her gaze darting to my lips.

Well, fuck. I briefly considered scrapping the rest of the date and going straight to my bedroom to try my luck a second time, but barely restrained myself when I heard the horse whinny.

Oh, that's right. Forgot to mention I'd booked a horse and carriage to take us to dinner. But not just any horse and carriage. The one sitting in front of my house was the *Cinderella* carriage, made of white bars and swirls in the shape of a pumpkin.

"Then let's get to dinner, huh?" I stepped back, still holding tight to her hand, to give her a better view of the carriage, and her reaction did not disappoint.

She gasped and her free hand went to her chest. Then a smile so radiant I'd be living off of it for days, lit up her face. She turned to me and that's when I knew that no matter how dinner went or how badly I bumbled the conversation, I had a chance. All the love I felt for her shined back at me through her eyes. We had things to discuss, for sure, but the feelings were there. Mutual. Unfiltered. No longer masked by fear.

I led the way, careful to keep my pace slow so she could navigate the curb and patch of grass in her stilettos and long dress. She giggled halfway there, a sound I'd never get tired of hearing. It was the grown-up version to Milly's giggle.

"Now I understand the suit." I spun my head, a question in the way my eyebrows climbed my forehead. "You know, you always dress formal with your slacks and sweaters, but even for you, the suit was a bit much for a casual Saturday."

"Ah, yes. You know it's a big deal when I don't wear my favorite sweaters. But I knew you'd be stunning in that dress, and a new suit seemed like the right thing. You're not mad I kept your afternoon activities a secret?"

We reached the carriage and I opened the door for her. She paused before stepping up.

"Mad? That you planned a whole day of activities to make me feel special? No, Jameson. I'm the opposite of mad."

I helped lift her up into the carriage and waited until she got her skirt situated before climbing up next to her. "You know I'm a science professor, right? I don't know the antonyms for mad."

She tossed back her head and laughed. "I'll just have to show you then." The sexy smirk on her face made the wind roar in my ears and my pants decidedly tighter.

"Oh, wait!" Lily-Marie nearly jumped off the bench seat. "I forgot something! Can you run into my house and grab the stapled papers off the breakfast table?"

I frowned, wondering what she could have that was so important. "Sure. Let me grab them. Here's a blanket if you're cold." I placed it on her lap and over her bare arms. Yes, it was Southern California, but it was also still February. Temperatures could get down into the fifties at night.

I ran into her house and found the papers easily, rushing out to climb back in the carriage. With a flick of the wrist, the horses were off, clopping down the street. I'd booked the entire Italian restaurant near our houses. A candlelit dinner for two and no one to bother us.

We were going slow enough that we barely passed a runner on the sidewalk. I did a double take and realized it was Runner Boy from the other day, off on another run without his shirt on. A deep smugness puffed up my chest, knowing she'd turned him down and here she was on a date with me instead.

Lily-Marie didn't even look at the passing scenery, just handed me her papers and then twisted the blanket in her lap.

"What's this?"

She twisted so she was looking right at me, worry etched across her face. "I'm sorry, Jameson. I've been meaning to say that for a while now. I'm sorry for walking away from you when you told me you loved me. You see, I realized I carry some baggage from my ex. And I let that taint what we have. Or had. I-I'm hoping this date tonight means you still want me."

I gave my head a shake. "Still want you? Lily-Marie, I want you always. Forever. I wasn't lying or confused or mistaken when I said I love you. I know I just blurted it out there and I should have done a better job of it, but as you know, words aren't my forte."

Lily-Marie rushed to interrupt. "No! It was perfect. Really. I just wasn't ready to hear it. That's all. Can you forgive me?"

I grabbed her hands, gently prying them off the blanket. "I already have. But I have something to confess before we go any further."

Her eyebrows drew together. "What do you mean?"

I squeezed her hands and laid it all out. "My father called

when we first moved here. Turns out he'd found some articles my grandmother had written a long time ago. She was an advice columnist for Prevention. He shared one with me that was called Fifty Ways to Find a Wife. I'd just had a conversation with Stein about love and I'd explained to him how I didn't think romantic love was a real thing. Biological love for offspring is documented, but I just didn't agree with love between non-related humans. I hadn't experienced it or really even seen it in my life, so I told him I'd prove it didn't exist. I took the article and tried out her list on you. We'd just met and I liked you, so you seemed like the perfect woman to try things out on."

"Oh my God." Lily-Marie had gone pale under her makeup. I rushed to keep going, to get out the whole story before she demanded to be taken home.

"No, but wait. Turns out, my hypothesis was incorrect. Massively. Romantic love definitely exists and when I realized that, I was so excited, I blurted out that I loved you at the wrong time. All those things I was trying from the article didn't make you fall in love with me, it helped me fall in love with *you*. But you're not an experiment. And I should have explained everything before I told you how I felt. You deserve more than an ill-timed confession of love blurted out while I had you pressed against the wall."

Her cheeks flushed with color again. "I quite liked being pressed against the wall." She squeezed my hands and lifted her legs to drape them across my lap. "Thank you for telling me. But I have my own confession and you're going to freak out when you hear it."

"You can tell me anything, I promise." I couldn't help myself. I flipped her long dress up and tunneled my hand underneath to stroke her bare leg.

"Mmm..." She closed her eyes for a second and then opened them. "Keep that up and I might start bumbling my words too." We smiled at each other. "I love to go to yard sales. Have I told you that? Well, I was at one right after you moved in and I found an old magazine I ended up buying. Guess the title of the column that caught my eye?"

At my headshake, she kept going. "Fifty Ways to Find a Husband, written by Loni Sanders in 1959."

My hand froze. "That's my grandmother. Well, that's her pen name. You read her article?"

She nodded, a grin creeping onto her face. "Yep. I sure did. And I followed it to a tee. I kept trying her list out on random men and you kept foiling my flirting."

I was shell-shocked. I literally couldn't believe what I was hearing. "So, the same list, but for women, that I was following too? Only you were attempting to flirt with other men, while I was attempting to flirt with you?"

She nodded, her grin now a giggle. "Can you believe that?"

"Breaking down in front of the firemen?"

"Part of the list."

"Baking pies? Making your own clothes?"

"The list." She tilted her head. "Dancing? Flowers?" She gasped. "The button on your shirt?"

"All from the list," I confirmed with a nod. "What are the odds that we'd move right next to each other and both find an old article of my grandmother's from 1959 about finding a partner and actually follow through with it?"

"The odds have to be pretty high. Probably more than winning the lottery."

"It's like it was..."

"Fate?" she whispered.

"Destiny," I answered.

19

ily-Marie

Dinner was a heady rush of intimate conversation, long glances, and a new feeling flooding my body I couldn't quite put my finger on. His focus was 100 percent on me and me alone. The attention was like rain in the desert, necessary, wanted, treasured. But I almost couldn't absorb it all. I was in my head, wondering what I'd done to deserve this man. I wanted to stop thinking and just feel, just appreciate this time with him.

He'd rented out an entire restaurant for me, delivered me there in a horse-drawn carriage, and attended to my every need. Well, except for one. I was hoping he'd satisfy that one later tonight too.

When we'd stuffed ourselves on the best ravioli and tiramisu, Jameson pushed back his chair and dropped his napkin on his empty plate. Our server didn't even come out with a bill, which was weird, but I guess when renting out a whole restaurant, that's taken care of ahead of time. I wouldn't know about such things. I only had the disposable income to rent out a Taco Bell in the early morning hours when there wasn't much demand for a bean burrito anyway.

He came around, his eyes morphing into a darker gray that spoke right to the pulse between my legs. I shoved back my chair before he could get to it, nearly tipping it over in my haste to get to the rest of the evening's entertainment.

His low chuckle vibrated right through me, shaking me out of my head and finally returning me to my body. Then his hands skated up my arms from behind, causing goose bumps to follow.

"I miss your hair," he whispered as he kissed along the back of my neck.

"Pretty sure it's still there..." My voice came out breathy and I was happy our waiter wasn't there to hear how far gone I already was.

That low chuckle again. "Oh, it's there, Rapunzel. I just want it down so I can wrap it around my fist and tug on it."

Holy fucknuts, Jameson was talking dirty to me. My mouth went dry and all the moisture went south. I loved how he could go from a nerdy professor in conversation to a dirty-talking Don Juan mere seconds later.

"Let's go home." He pulled away and I shivered again, missing the warmth that radiated from his muscled torso. Holding my hand, he walked us out to the carriage and wrapped a blanket around my shoulders and another across my lap.

As the horse lurched into motion, he palmed my cheek and tilted my head just where he wanted it. His lips touched mine with an urgency that surpassed our previous make-out session, a level I didn't think was possible.

Not much was said on the way home, at least not with words. We'd said everything we needed to say at dinner. God willing, the rest of the evening would be about feeling, touching, fucking. Please, please, please let there be fucking.

By the time we reached my house, I was ready to strip down there in the carriage for all our neighbors to see. Everything was on fire and I'd lost all inhibitions.

Jameson pulled away and stood up, hitting his head on the carriage. I giggled, giddy to see his tented suit pants, knowing he was just as turned on as I was. He lifted an eyebrow at my laughter and even that was working for me.

We practically ran out of the carriage and up to my house, not even saying thank you to our sweet driver. I sure hoped Jameson would tip him well.

"Hold on, let me take off my heels." I tugged on his hand to get him to slow down.

"Nope. I have visions of those on my shoulders. Here." Dipping down, Jameson ignored my yelp and scooped me up in a princess carry, proceeding to race to my front door and open it with my keys.

See what I meant about Don Juan? He just said he wanted my stilettos on his shoulders and I was ready to combust with lust. How did a nerdy science teacher learn to talk so perfectly raunchy?

"How many women have you been with?" I asked in wonder.

Jameson got us inside, slammed the door shut, and flipped the lock. I could just make out his face in the light from the porch.

"Are you sure you want to ask that right now?"

I realized his meaning and shook my head. "Nope, pretty sure I don't care. Just wanted to know how you learned to talk like that."

He smiled, more than a hint of wickedness in it. "You like when I talk dirty, huh?"

"I fucking love it."

"Tsk, tsk. Such a mouth for a princess."

I laid my hand on his cheek, loving the rough stubble that scraped my skin. "I love princess movies and I know I've always wanted to be swept off my feet, but I realized I don't actually need that. I'm no princess, stuck in some ridiculous fairy tale with unrealistic expectations." My heart lurched in my chest. "Wait! Do you still have my papers?"

I'd completely forgotten my intent from this morning: to write an essay showing Jameson that I loved him back. He kept walking, moving us through my living room and up the stairs.

"They're in my jacket pocket. Which way?" He nodded down the hall.

"Oh, the door at the end." I pushed aside his jacket lapel and fished around for a pocket in the lining. His muscles jumped as I felt him up. I almost abandoned my mission for more feeling up, but the maturity gained by being in my thirties slowed me down and helped me focus.

"Aha!" I pulled it out right as he dumped me on my bed. I went with the bounce and then scrambled up to my elbows.

I looked up from my papers to see him take off his suit jacket and throw it on a chair. His eyes were hooded with desire, which just fed mine. "As much as I love what's happening right now, I need to read this to you first."

His jaw twitched, but he nodded. "Better make it quick."

I gulped. This alpha male thing he had going on was unbelievably hot. Unexpected, even after our make-out session. Then he unhooked his belt and slid it out of the loops ever so slowly. His look was clear: say what I needed to say while he stripped for me. I wasn't sure that was even humanly possible. How could I read this stupid essay when my eyes had better things to do?

I cleared my throat. "Okay, so this seemed more important this morning, but I wrote you an essay." He didn't say a thing, just toed off his shoes.

"Here goes." I proceeded in a wavering voice to read all the scientific findings about love and where scientists said it came from. I paused to hazard a glance up, which rewarded me with the sight of his shirt completely unbuttoned. Then he whipped it off his shoulders, pulling at the cuffs, his muscles bunching and flexing in the dim light from the small bedside lamp.

I sucked in a deep breath and decided to rush through the rest and get to the point. "So, basically, they say the symptoms of being in love are breathlessness, a tugging sensation in the chest, exhilaration, euphoria, a racing heart, increased energy, and sleeplessness. All of which I've experienced in regards to you." I fluttered my eyes back up to him, his hands frozen on his waistband, suspended in the act of taking them off.

We stared at each other for several long beats. "Say something, please," I whispered. I could barely get the words past my throat. I was scared. I was ashamed. Had he felt like this when he told me he loved me? I just ran out on him. I had no idea how he was able to survive my callousness.

If he turned me down right now, I might just disintegrate into the air. Cease to exist without his affirmation. Refuse to stay here on this plane of reality where he didn't love me back. What kind of heartless bitch was I the other day?

"Are you saying you love me?" His words came out slow and measured. His body didn't move. I wasn't sure he even breathed.

I swallowed. "Yes. I know so. I love you, Jameson."

He unfroze, lunging toward me, his hands digging into my hair to frame my face.

"I love you too, Lily-Marie. So much." Then his mouth was crushing me, crushing the essay between our bodies. He was wild, lost in this moment with me.

Then he was gone.

The cold air hit me and I opened my eyes to see him standing upright again, shoving his pants down his legs. Then his boxers and socks. The scene was like a present being opened slowly, the wrapping paper carefully peeled back and folded when all I wanted to do was rip it all off and consume my gift.

Those legs I'd wanted to touch when I'd seen him in his cycling shorts that first day. Those smoldering gray eyes that said

I was his everything no matter what ridiculous thing I happened to be doing. That dark hair I couldn't wait to run my fingers through and mess up. The abs I'd counted in the dressing room for the first time, amazed they were real.

It was all a gift. Just for me. Jameson was mine.

His cock stole the show, bobbing as he stalked back to me, its tip brushing against his stomach. My thighs clenched in anticipation, becoming so very needy. He was beautiful.

"Stand up." He stood at the foot of the bed, palming his dick, so sure I'd follow his command.

Which was smart, because, let's get real. What woman wouldn't follow his orders right now? I'd do lots of questionable things to get my hands and mouth on that cock tonight.

I tossed the essay over the side of the bed and scooted over to stand as quickly as possible, now toe to toe with Jameson. As badly as I wanted to reach for him, I kept my hands by my sides, wanting to see what else would come out of that mouth of his.

"Turn around."

Turning, he unzipped my dress and helped it fall to the ground.

He paused and I could feel his gaze trailing down the length of my body, looking his fill. And more than ever, I wished I'd followed the one thing on my list I'd ignored: go on a diet. He was a specimen with all his easily identifiable muscles. I bet he was a hit in anatomy class in college: a living, breathing diagram. And then there was me, a mom of two with socially unacceptable curves and lumps and stretch marks. My only saving grace was I'd bought a black lace thong and bra this afternoon on the urging of my best friend.

"No pink underwear?" Jameson's voice was barely above a rumble, a hint of disappointment that had me confused.

"Huh?"

"That day in your home-sewn skirt. You flashed me and you

had on pink cotton underwear. Do you have any idea how many fantasies I've had with you in that pair of underwear?"

A rush of warmth filled me, transforming me into a goddess who straightened her spine and pushed out her breasts with pride. "I don't know why you say you have a problem with words. You say the absolute most perfect things."

A fingertip started at my neck, traced down my spine, unhooked my bra, and kept traveling south to the lacy scrap at my hip. I felt his touch all the way down to my toes.

Thumbs hooked into the sides of my thong and tugged downward. "Step out."

As he crouched down behind me, I did just that, also allowing my bra to slide off my arms to lie in a heap with my dress. He pressed his face to each of my thighs, his lips and tongue gliding their way back up my body. I shivered and gasped.

I expected his hands to find their way to my breasts, but instead, Jameson detoured to my hair, rapidly pulling out pins and tossing them to the floor until my hair cascaded down my back.

"Finally," he muttered, his hands brushing through the long strands. "Sit on the edge of the bed."

I turned and sat, aware of the close proximity of my mouth to his straining cock. I wanted a taste, just a small taste, but when I bent forward, Jameson pulled back and shook his head.

He dipped to his knees and pulled my knees apart. And then he knelt there, just looking his fill. I was embarrassed by his stare, but also incredibly turned on by it.

He glanced up, eyes so very dark. "I want to worship your body. Can I do that, princess?"

Before I could answer, he dipped his head, his broad shoulders spreading my legs farther. He dove in like a man possessed, his tongue and mouth working me over with no reprieve. A deep groan reverberated through me and I flopped back onto the bed. I was limp, all nerve endings having left their job stations to run between my legs and get in on the action.

A thick finger entered me, followed by a second, filling me and making me burn for more. An orgasm was right there on the edge of my attention, ramping up speed and power, waiting to decimate.

But Jameson had other ideas. He pulled out and stood up. I blinked rapidly, trying to catch up and figure out where the hell he went. I found him staring down at me, spread eagle on the bed, sucking on his fingers. A fierce blush spread across my cheeks.

He popped his fingers out and barked out more orders. "Stand up on the bed."

"Huh?" I was quite the linguist when close to orgasm.

He just tilted his head, daring me to follow his instructions. I was dazed, but not so confused that I didn't understand my orgasm hinged in the balance here. I scrambled inelegantly to my feet again—not an easy feat in stilettos—this time climbing up on the bed and standing there, waiting for more.

He came closer, laying his head on my stomach and pulling me into a hug. His head turned into me and his lips plucked at my skin, no doubt leaving marks I'd treasure tomorrow. Then he picked me up and I wrapped my legs around his waist. He carried me over to the opposite wall, spinning until he pinned me there.

"Birth control?" he murmured between kisses.

"Yes."

Then he lowered me down, slamming into me in one stroke.

I gasped from the intrusion. There was so much to take in. And it had been so long.

"Goddammit. I'm sorry." His face was twisted into a grimace, his eyes squeezed tight.

"You didn't hurt me. Just surprised," I managed to reply.

"Mhmm..." He began to move, his hips pinning me against the wall while his mouth found its way down my neck.

I tried to hang on, but there wasn't much need for it. Jameson was in control and he had no chance of letting me go. He moved me where he wanted me, tilting my hips with his big hands, setting the pace. I was simply along for the ride.

And ride I did, right to the end when an orgasm was so front and center it was the only thing I knew, the only thing I saw. It consumed me, freezing my limbs locked around Jameson. His name stumbled past my lips, a new chant I never wanted to stop saying.

I chased the light until the room came back to me. Jameson's hand pulled my head back down so I was looking at him. "I need to see you, beautiful." He plunged back in once, twice, then on the third, he trembled. His mouth opened like he was going to say something, but no sound came out. His gray eyes clouded over and I watched it all with a front row seat, a heady feeling knowing I'd made this big man weak as a puppy.

Long moments later, when our breathing was under control, I couldn't stop touching him. I wanted my hands on every muscle all at once, so I petted him like the obsessed woman I was.

He finally chuckled. "Figured we needed to finish what we started the other day. The wall was good to us."

I couldn't wipe the smile from my face. "Agreed, and I didn't slide down this time."

"There's still time for that," he teased me.

"Ha-ha. You've got me, right?"

He turned serious in a heartbeat, gaze burrowing into mine. "I've always got you, Lily-Marie."

Ah, shit, there went my heart, squeezing and sighing in my chest. "I know you do." I was so happy I thought I'd burst. "I think you found a fifty-first way to find a wife. Order her around in the bedroom."

He threw his head back and laughed. I wanted to make him do that every day. "Are you asking me to marry you, Ms. Masters?"

I swatted his arms of steel. "Oh you shush, that's not what I meant."

He kept laughing, sliding out of me and helping me to my feet. "Yeah, I know, but teasing you makes your cheeks pink and that's one of my favorite things about you."

I felt thoroughly ravished, yet here we were, teasing each other while still naked, his release sliding down my inner thighs. "I thought my pink underwear was your favorite thing?"

He smacked me on my bare ass as he walked to the bed, pulling back the covers. "I have about a thousand things about you that are my favorites. Get in bed and I'll take your heels off."

Oh, the ordering around was back and damn if I didn't jump to do his bidding. He made quick work of my shoes and pulled me into him.

He gave me a smug smile as we snuggled under the covers. "See? Another one of my favorite things. You do as I say."

I trailed my hand down his six-pack, then lower, finding him delightfully hard again. "Only when you use that voice."

And then he proceeded to use that voice all night long.

20

ameson

Sun was already filtering through Lily-Marie's blinds by the time I woke the next morning. Her scent, that hint of lemon and something else I couldn't place, surrounded me like an onshore fog as I lay in her bed. Memories of last night filled my brain, making me happier than I'd ever been.

Lily-Marie loved me.

She'd written a goddamn essay to tell me how much. It meant the world to me to know she'd truly thought about me and told me how she felt in the way she thought I'd most understand and appreciate. I could only hope she felt the same way with the plans I'd executed for her last night.

Her head was lying in the crook of my arm, her breath fanning my chest as she exhaled. That long blond hair was strewn over her back, my arm, and the pillow, covering every surface with its silk. My body tightened painfully just remembering how I'd wrapped that hair around my fist at one point during the night and taken her from behind. I'd whispered into her ear exactly what I wanted her to do and without even a blink of an eye, she'd obeyed.

Gently grabbing the hand that lay on my stomach, I lowered her palm to my cock without waking her, loving the sight of her pale skin against mine. Turning my head, I glanced at the clock, seeing it was almost nine. Stein, Clark, and Milly would all be home by eleven, so we needed to get up and get our day started. Surprisingly, both my ex and Lily-Marie's ex had been cordial when I called asking for a favor. They'd both agreed to the overnight, thus allowing us one precious night without the kids around so I could make my grand gesture.

I nuzzled my nose into Lily-Marie's neck, kissing her earlobe and then that pulsing beat behind her jaw. Her moan told me she was awake, even if her eyes hadn't opened yet. Her hand flexed on my cock, stealing my breath.

"Wake up, sleepyhead."

"Shush. I'm having a really good sex dream right now. There's this hot guy kissing my neck and you oughta see the size of his —*beaker*," she whispered, sounding more and more breathless.

I smiled into her neck. "Did you just make a science joke?"

"Maybe you should *experiment* and see."

I barely contained the snort. This woman was amazing in every way. "You should totally climb on top and *bond* with him."

She finally opened her eyes, the blue orbs the prettiest thing I'd seen in the morning. "Don't mind if I do."

And then she rolled, her knees going to each side of my waist. Without hesitation she lifted up and fitted my cock to her entrance, sliding down ever so slowly.

She gasped. I hissed. Sweet torture.

She leaned forward, placing her hands on the pillow on either side of my head, and began to move. My hands found their way to her hips, needing more of her skin against me as she lit up my body with each slide. Her breasts smashed against my chest and her hair created a tent around us, making me feel like I was in a cocoon with only her and me. The outside world didn't exist when we were connected like this.

Lily-Marie's groans picked up volume and I knew she was close. When she switched to my name and her hips faltered in their rhythm, I took over, jackhammering up into her. She tumbled over the edge just seconds before me. Sealing our lips together, we clung on tight until the tremors subsided.

"Good morning, Professor," she said brightly from my chest, where her face was buried.

"Good morning, princess."

When we finally made it out of bed, we agreed to get showered and dressed at our respective houses even though being apart even for an hour wasn't what I wanted. The plan was to meet back at Lily-Marie's house and we'd be together when the kids came home. We'd sit them down and tell them we were dating, but we agreed no spending the night. Not yet. We wanted to ease them into the dating idea to make sure they were comfortable with it.

After too many long kisses goodbye, she finally pushed me out the door and I went back to my house to shower. I was loath to wash her scent off me so soon, but being a good parent came first. My one night with Lily-Marie would not be my last. In fact, if the ring I squirreled away in the back of my sock drawer was any indication, I intended for it to be the first of forever.

During my week of preparation for my grand gesture, I'd contemplated asking her to marry me, but finally chose against it. I'd blurted out "I love you" way too soon and she'd run. I wasn't going to make the same mistake twice. Plus, the kids needed time to adjust to this new relationship first.

But I'd bought the ring, knowing it was an inevitability. The ring had a platinum setting with diamonds all along the band. In a stroke of fate, I'd used my grandmother's princess cut diamond in the setting, thinking her list of fifty ways had brought me to Lily-Marie. Now I knew her list of fifty ways had also brought Lily-Marie to me in a roundabout way. It only made sense for her to wear my grandmother's diamond.

I'd just toweled off from my shower when my phone rang. I ran to it, thinking it might be Lily-Marie or even Stein, but saw my father's number on the screen instead. I picked it up.

"Hey, Dad, can I call you back this afternoon?"

"Son! Actually, I have to share something really quick first. You know that article of your grandmother's I sent you? The one about finding a wife?" He started wheezing and I rolled my eyes. Better to put him on speakerphone and keep getting dressed. This could take a while.

He finally wound the wheeze up enough to let out a few loud guffaws and finally actual words. "I found another one...get this...Fifty Ways to Catch a Cheating Husband." He dissolved into a fit of laughter again before sobering enough to continue. "One of the ways she listed? Poke holes in his condoms and soak in peppermint oil."

He let out a loud shout and then it sounded like he put the phone down to laugh it out, probably bent over, slapping his knee. I couldn't help but crack a smile at his antics. This guy loved a reason to laugh, and apparently, my grandmother's articles were gold mines.

Maybe it was a good thing I didn't launch into my experiment with Grandmother's list the minute I answered the phone. He would've laughed me off the phone, or worse, come to my front door to laugh at me in person and check if I was feverish.

"Okay, Dad, I gotta go." I talked loudly into the speaker of the phone, hoping he could hear me over his laughter.

"I mean—who the hell would follow this loon's advice?"

Another wave of laughter rippled through the phone and I shouted to be heard, my face heating. He could never find out I'd followed her list. It would be too mortifying.

"Gotta go, love you." I hung up and made a mental note to tell Lily-Marie about my father and ensure her secrecy. A big, mushy grin took hold of my face at the thought of introducing Lily-Marie to my father. They'd get along great, I just knew it.

Gelling my hair back and washing my hands completed my getting ready. It was time to get back to Lily-Marie and talk to our kiddos. I ran out the door and barely made it inside before she was there in front of me, beautiful in one of her dresses that drove me crazy.

"How did you get ready before me, huh?" I didn't know how she did it. She looked freshly showered and ready for her day, but I thought women always took longer to get ready.

She scoffed at me. "I'm a single mom. I know all the tricks." She ticked them off on her fingers. "Dry shampoo, minimal makeup, dresses that don't require ironing, strong coffee. Simple really."

I shook my head slowly, pulling her into me and wrapping my arms around her. "You're amazing."

The front door flew open and hit the opposite wall with a bang. We jumped apart and saw Milly standing there with a big grin on her face. Clark was slowly coming up the walkway behind her and I saw my ex's car pulling up to the curb.

"Mommy! Guess what? My tooph is wiggly!" Milly ran right up to us and pushed a front lower tooth with her tongue, and sure enough, the sucker was just barely moving.

Lily-Marie got down on her knees and held Milly's face, her jaw dropped and eyes sparkling.

"Oh my gosh, my big girl! I'm so proud of you." She gave her a hug and then Milly was dancing over to me, her tongue pushing on her tooth, so proud of her achievement.

"Ewww, that's so gross. I can't look!" I feigned disgust and she let out a peal of giggles.

"Come here and look at my tooph, mister!" She chased me and I ran in circles in the living room, finally letting her catch me and wiggle her tooth right in my face.

"Hey, buddy. Stay down here, would ya?" Lily-Marie stopped Clark from going upstairs to his room.

Stein hovered at the door, wondering if it was okay to just come into Lily-Marie's house.

"Come on in, Stein. Your father and I would like to chat with you three." Lily-Marie pulled him into the house with an arm around his shoulders, closing the door and leaving the five of us to talk.

Taking the lead, I waved us over to the couches and we all sat, Stein and Clark looking at each other with wide-eyed faces then flickering a glance at us. Milly just sat there and wiggled her tooth.

"Okay, you all know Lily-Marie and I went on a date last night. I'm sure you're wondering how it went"—Clark groaned and I managed to contain my chuckle—"while also not really wanting to know the details. So, I'm happy to say that we're now officially dating."

I held Lily-Marie's hand and the kids' gazes darted around, not sure how to react or who to take their cues from.

Stein finally stood up and gave me a hug. "Nicely done, Dad. I'm glad you're done with your experiment and dating Lily-Marie." Then he gave Lily-Marie a hug and Clark jumped up to do the same, opting to give me a fist pump instead of a hug.

The boys started talking amongst themselves and then went out back to play. Milly sat on the couch opposite us and kept wiggling her tooth, no expression whatsoever.

"Do you have any questions for Mommy?" Lily-Marie asked her.

She hopped off the couch and wrinkled her forehead. "Do I get another daddy?"

I gulped, the only reaction I allowed, even though I wanted to cry like a baby and wrap her in a hug.

"Yes, love, you get two daddies for now," Lily-Marie spoke softly.

"Forever." I nodded at Milly and she finally unfroze and rushed over to me. I gave her a big hug, memorizing the feel of her little arms around my neck. Lily-Marie might need some more time to get used to the idea of forever, but Milly and I were already there.

~

The Reality of Love, Mom-Com Style - episode #10

All good things must come to an end, dear reader. Fortunately, that doesn't mean an end for our girl, Betty. Just an end to her quest to find Mr. Perfect. He's been found, they've swept each other off their feet, and they are currently living happily ever after.

It's a tale as old as time: boy meets girl, girl tries ridiculously old-fashioned things to find a husband, and boy blocks her attempts and swoops in to steal her heart.

We have also learned that the modern Prince Charming is, in fact, quite muscular, handsome, and dashing, but can also be found in the nerdy professor living next door.

Some may say that the list of ways to find a husband worked like a charm. Others might say love was found in spite of the list of ways. Either way, if you drop your handkerchief and a man picks it up, you may want to get his number.

EPILOGUE

Two Years Later

Gabby

I didn't want to say "I told them so," but...I totally told them so. I called that. Should have placed money on the bet. The two love-birds were the real deal. They were going to make it in a sea of failed relationships and broken promises.

I was over at Lily-Marie's house—or should I say Lily-Marie and Jameson's house, as they'd moved in together last year when they got engaged—enjoying their co-ed baby shower. They didn't want to do a girls-only baby shower and have to be apart for the afternoon. I know, how sickly sweet was that shit?

Anyway, I agreed to host the baby shower and had spent weeks planning games, party favors, decorations, and meal plan-ning. Nothing was too much for my girl, Lil. Now that it was basi-cally over with just a few stragglers porch lighting, I could sit back and enjoy the fruits of my labor in the form of a stacked plate of barbecue ribs and cake. Might have seemed like an odd combination, but it was delightfully sinful.

And I needed some sin. God, yes, I needed something sweet after the world's nastiest breakup and subsequent dry spell. Just as Lily-Marie was reaching the pinnacle of happiness by having her hot boyfriend propose to her at the happiest place on earth, I was experiencing the deepest valley of depression. Obviously, I swore off all men after catching my fiancé of five years cheating on me with his boss. It had been a long year.

I was getting restless. Maybe a little baby-crazy watching Lily-Marie pop out a third human being while I was stretch-mark-less at the ripe old age of thirty-four. Or maybe it was the beautiful princess cut diamond on her finger that blinded me on the regular.

Some might say I was jealous, but I so wasn't. I was envious.

Big difference.

Jealousy would make me petty and mean-spirited. And I wasn't. I just wanted everything she had for myself.

I bit into the juicy rib meat, ripping it off the bone and nearly moaning from the sauce's flavor bursting in my mouth. A head or two swiveled in my direction, but I didn't care. Etiquette meant I should apologize for making a public display of eating my food, but it was as close to an orgasm as I'd be getting any time soon, so those judge-y fuckers should cut me some slack.

Jameson was leaning against the back wall of the house leisurely talking to some friends, his arms around Lily-Marie, his thumb absentmindedly stroking her belly. He leaned forward and nuzzled into her neck, whispering something to make her blush and start giggling.

They were adorable. He'd proposed and they'd gotten married two weeks later right here in this backyard, Milly the flower girl and the two boys the groomsmen. I'd been the maid of honor, looking like a skeleton in my satin dress. I'd discovered that heartache killed one's appetite.

No one had been looking at me anyway, not with Lily-Marie in her white wedding dress that rivaled any princess, real or in the movies. Six months after they started dating, she'd found the dress, begging me to keep it at my house so Jameson wouldn't know about it and feel pressured into proposing. She'd glowed on her wedding day like she had the world at her feet, which she did. Jameson doted on her like it was his life's purpose. Even the kids had been angels that day, wanting their parents to have true love together. The whole thing was a goddamn fairy tale.

I finished my last rib, licking my fingers clean before using one of the wet wipes I'd liberally strewn over the picnic table for the guests. More dirty looks, but I wasn't going to let one drop of that barbecue sauce go to waste. I wasn't a quitter.

Grabbing my fork, I eyed the huge square of cake I'd cut for myself. Did I mention I'd lost a lot of weight after the breakup? Well, I had some making up to do. Some may think I was having a close brush with gluttony, but really, I was just looking out for my health.

See, I had a plan.

My newspaper job put me in contact with many interesting people in the entertainment industry. At the suggestion of an acquaintance from years ago, I'd been approached last week to be part of a new show called Real Househusbands. It was a reality show where they followed around couples where the woman was the breadwinner and the househusbands led interesting lives doing whatever unemployed rich people did all day.

I know you're sitting there thinking there's one little problem: I didn't have a husband.

Yes, I know, but when opportunity knocks, you don't give all the reasons why you can't do it. You say yes and then scramble to figure that shit out.

I had three weeks until they started their interviews of the couples. Three weeks to find a husband. Three weeks to show the world my life wasn't a total wreck. Three weeks to present a new, sparkling reality and shove my happiness down my ex's throat.

Revenge would be so sweet.

If Lily-Marie could find a husband with a sexist 1950s list of ways to trap a man, I was sure I could pay a guy to act as my husband for a few months of filming. Weirder things had happened. Once I'd made my ex jealous, I'd finally be able to move on, find a real husband, and ride off into the sunset together. Easy-peasy.

Right?

NOTE FROM THE AUTHOR

Thank you so much for reading Mom-Com! If you loved it, please support the series by leaving a review on Amazon or Goodreads so other readers can find it and enjoy it too. Reviews help other readers determine if a book is to their liking and they help indie authors sell more books so we can keep writing. If you hated it, please disregard this entire paragraph. :)

If you'd like to know more about me or the other novels that I'm writing, please come stalk find me on Facebook, or my private Reader Group, or you can find me in-person, on the beach in Southern California, frolicking like a Baywatch babe.

I'm everywhere....
Amazon - https://www.amazon.com/author/marikaray

Goodreads - https://www.goodreads.com/author/show/16856659.Marika_Ray

Bookbub - https://www.bookbub.com/authors/marika-ray

Note From the Author

Instagram - https://www.instagram.com/authormarikaray

Twitter - https://www.twitter.com/authormarikaray

Pinterest - https://www.pinterest.com/marikarayauthor/

Book + Main - https://bookandmainbites.com/MarikaRay

READING ORDER

<u>Urban Fantasy Trilogy</u>:
1) The Cult Queen (as part of the Prophesy of Magic anthology) - PreOrder Now for 99cents!
2) The Cult Queen's Court
3) The Cult Queen's Revenge

CLOSING COSTS PROLOGUE

I slammed the door shut behind me and let out a heavy sigh. I should be jubilant. Hell, I should be out drinking and celebrating. Instead, I was nearly sick to my stomach at the thought of moving. I'd just come back from a hard run, trying to work the nerves out of my system.

I'd gotten the news about the new job in San Francisco a week ago and I still hadn't told my best friend, Austin. We'd grown up together and we still lived together a year after graduating college. The future was bright, but in order to embrace it, I had to move a few hundred miles away from the guy who was more a brother than a friend. I couldn't very well start showing up at our apartment with moving boxes without him questioning what the hell was going on.

I tossed my keys on the kitchen counter and yanked my sweat soaked shirt up over my head. I needed a shower. And then I needed to pull my balls down from wherever they'd been hiding and tell Austin the news. My socks and shoes got stripped off next, leaving a messy trail I'd need to clean up later.

I swung open my bedroom door and froze.

Lying there on my bed was Austin's little sister, Abi.

Her long blonde hair was fanned over my pillow as she lay on her side. Her eyes were closed, her chest rising and falling with each breath. She only wore a tiny tank top which left her breasts nearly spilling out of the low neckline.

I swore under my breath and averted my eyes. Unfortunately, that had me looking at her bottom half, the long shapely tan legs that went on for miles. The denim shorts she wore were way too short for her age. She'd just turned seventeen, going on thirty. She didn't have the parental supervision she needed living in foster care.

Austin would have a fit knowing she was in that outfit.

And because I couldn't keep my eyes off her.

She was never a nuisance growing up. I'd always felt like she was my sister too. I was her protector just as much as Austin was, but lately when I thought about her, it was turning into so much more than that for me.

Out of respect for Austin I'd kept my distance from Abi this last year, something that I think hurt her feelings, but we never talked about it. Then Austin and Abi's mom got sick and passed away not long ago. Abi had fallen apart and I'd broken my rule of three feet of distance at all times. She needed me and I could put my feelings aside long enough to be there for her.

Just the sight of her asleep on my bed was enough to have my body hardening. I couldn't do this.

"She's like a sister," I kept repeating in my head, though my body knew the truth.

Her eyes fluttered open and when she saw me in the doorway, she bolted upright.

"Marcos." She looked so soft and warm and quite a bit lost sitting there. I wanted to go to her, but I willed my feet to stay where they were.

When I didn't move or respond, she hopped off the bed and slowly walked toward me. My heart raced, my brain warring with myself on what I wanted to do. When she was only a foot away, she smacked a sheet of paper on my chest, startling me.

I looked down and saw the formal acceptance letter from the real estate firm in San Francisco.

"What the hell is this?" She accused me with her eyes.

I grabbed the paper out of her hand and threw it down on my desk. "I haven't told Austin yet, so you need to keep quiet."

She came even closer and I could smell her. Shampoo and perfume.

Abi's hand flew and she slapped me. The sting on my cheek cleared my head in an instant.

"What the hell what that for?"

"You're leaving? Just like that?" She wasn't yelling, but her words lashed me anyway. I winced, knowing my absence would hurt her. It was for the best, she just couldn't see that yet.

I put my hands on her arms, steadying her. "I have to take it. I have—"

Her hands lifted and traced down my chest and over my abs, stealing away whatever I'd planned to say. She'd never touched me like that before.

"Abi..." I warned, my lungs on fire, my body already craving her now that I knew her touch.

She shook her head at me, those big blue eyes filled with tears, the anger gone. Then she pulled me into her and her lips were on mine.

Everything froze and zeroed in on her skin against mine, her lips moving over mine. Her tongue darted out to lick my bottom lip and everything unfroze in an instant. I wrapped my arms around her back and lifted her up, my mouth parting her lips.

I was out of my mind.

I needed more. So much more.

So even though a part of me knew this would only lead to disaster, I took.

My heartbeat thrummed up through my chest and into my head, blocking out all rational thought. It was just her and I, her breasts smashed against my chest, her little moans ringing in my ears, urging me on. She tasted like chocolate and freedom, a dangerous combination that should have pulled me to my senses. Instead, she wrapped her legs around my waist and I felt her heat. I could feel how much she wanted me and I knew she felt me growing in my shorts. I ground my cock against her jean shorts, the relief mild and short lived.

With lips still fused together, teeth clashing clumsily and gasps of breath between us, I turned and slammed her against the wall of my bedroom. She let out a mewl of pain that stopped me in my tracks.

I reared back my head, my heart dropping to my feet. Her lips were already red and swollen, wet from my tongue. Her eyes popped open, unfocused and confused. My hips thrust against her core one last time, against my will, seeking what I'd already decided I could never have.

What the hell did I just do?

I stepped back and pushed her legs down my body, disengaging from her even as she tried to cling to me.

"Marcos?" She looked at me, her eyes flooding with tears again.

"You're seventeen, Abi. You're my best friend's sister," I managed to gasp.

I ran both hands through my hair, wondering why I felt like I was ripping my heart straight out of my chest. "This never happened. Do you hear me?"

Her mouth dropped open like she wanted to argue. Instead, her face crumbled and she ran out the door without a word.

Closing Costs - Reality of Love #3 - Releasing in 2019